MAY THESE LEADEN BATTLEGROUNDS
LEAVE NO TRACE

Bullet Magic and Gho...

AIR ARLAND NOAH

MW00775035

A girl who
introduced
herself as
a Ghost of
the Belial
race. Boasts
overwhelming
combat prowess
and is the
creator of the
Devil's Bullet.

An elite officer
cadet from the
eastern country
of O'ltmenia.
The day he
obtained the
Devil's Bullet,
the cogs of fate
began to turn.

THE DEVIL'S BULLET

Holds the power of Oblivion.
Erases the existence and all the
achievements of whomever it
hits, Reprogramming and shifting
the history of the world...

ORCA DANDALOS

ATHLY MAGMET

A bright, cheerful female officer cadet. A talented Exelia manipulator who forms a first-class tag team with Rain.

Possessing superior fighting prowess and serving as something of a leader, he functions as Alestra Academy's prefect for Rain's class year.

"You've... wanted to tell me...something important... for a while now...? Is it... about you and me...? And our relationship... going forward?"

"You can beat the stuffing out of anyone who pisses you off, no problem!"

"You're trying to end this war, right? ...Interesting."

KIRLILITH LAMBERT

ALEC THANDA

A Ghost of the Oud race and an officer of the western country of Harborant. His confusing attitude makes it hard for others to realize his true intentions.

"If everything around us is evil, then I'll change every last bit of it."

The Ghost of the Traxil race. Possesses a bullet capable of inflicting death on anything it shoots, be it a living creature or an inanimate object.

"We're both Ghosts. I could never forget the face of an enemy I've fought for so long."

"In my eyes, wars and countries are but a means to live. A policy, a process...nothing more..."

"I am Air, a Ghost.
I'm not sure what
your definition of
human is,
but I've still got my
legs. See?"

...Air said as she rolled up her skirt.

"...You said...you'd change the world, didn't you?

Then your only path forward is to aim and shoot, Rain Lantz!"

MECHANICAL DESIGN:
NAOHIRO WASHIO

EXELIA — M4

EXELIA: EASTERN COUNTRY OF O'LTMENIA MODEL
[M4]

A two-person armored vehicle to be mounted by a manipulator and a gunner. The M4 was developed as a relatively easy to produce all-purpose unit and currently functions as the standard unit of the East. Despite its light weight and small size, it's remarkable for its armor, which is indestructible even in the harshest of environments.

Exelias are typically difficult to drive, but the M4's ease of use allows even new recruits to board it with minimal training. But on the other hand, since it's been used for many years, its viable tactics have been thoroughly researched, making it weak on the intelligence front. As a result, its military gains have been poor over the past few years.

SPECIFICATIONS

Total height:	**10.70 ft**
Total length:	**9.35 ft**
Full width:	**8.89 ft** (when parked)
Dry weight:	**884 lb**
Engine:	oil-cooled in-line four-cylinder 190 ps reciprocating engine

EXELIA: WESTERN COUNTRY OF HARBORANT MODEL
[AT3]

EXELIA — AT3

SPECIFICATIONS

Total height:	**11.98 ft**
Total length:	**12.47 ft**
Full width:	**9.74 ft** (when parked)
Dry weight:	**1,098 lb**
Engine:	water-cooled V-type six-cylinder 250 ps reciprocating engine

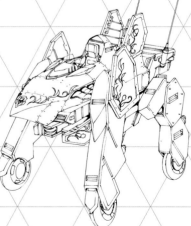

The West's state-of-the-art Exelia model. Its development concept was "a unit optimized for Exelia combat." Quadruped-wheeled models have an inherent design flaw that inhibits their ability to move in reverse, which the AT3 compensates for and conquers through engine output and an emphasis on maneuverability. The AT3 proved its superiority within a mere seventy days of its introduction to the battlefield, setting a precedent for future models.

Its production output is currently small, but thanks to the large amount of graimar nuclear alloy taken from the East, the West is poised to go into mass production of the AT3 model.

MAY THESE LEADEN BATTLEGROUNDS

LEAVE NO TRACE

Bullet Magic and Ghost Programs

VOL. I

KEI UEKAWA

ILLUSTRATION BY
TEDDY

MECHANICAL DESIGN BY
NAOHIRO WASHIO

YEN
ON

New York

Kei Uekawa

Translation by Roman Lempert
Yen On edition edited by Maneesh Maganti & Yen Press Editorial
Cover art by TEDDY

UCHI NUKARETA SENJOU HA, SOKO DE KIETEIRO Vol. 1
-DANGAN MAHO TO GHOST PROGRAM-
©Kei Uekawa, TEDDY, Naohiro Washio 2019
First published in Japan in 2019 by KADOKAWA CORPORATION, Tokyo.
English translation rights arranged with KADOKAWA CORPORATION, Tokyo through
TUTTLE-MORI AGENCY, INC., Tokyo.

English translation © 2020 by Yen Press, LLC

First Yen On Edition: July 2020

Yen On is an imprint of Yen Press, LLC.
The Yen On name and logo are trademarks of Yen Press, LLC.

The publisher is not responsible for websites (or their content) that are not owned by the publisher.

Library of Congress Cataloging-in-Publication Data
Names: Uekawa, Kei, author. | TEDDY (Illustrator), artist. | Mishima, Kurone, 1991– artist. | Lempert, Roman, translator.
Title: May these leaden battlegrounds leave no trace / Kei Uekawa ; artists, TEDDY and Kurone Mishima ; translation by Roman Lempert.
Other titles: Uchinukareta senjō wa, soko de kieteiro. English
Description: First Yen On edition. | New York, NY : Yen On, 2020.
Identifiers: LCCN 2020005361 | ISBN 9781975310301 (v. 1 ; trade paperback)
Subjects: CYAC: Fantasy.
Classification: LCC PZ7.1.U27 May 2020 | DDC [Fic]—dc23
LC record available at https://lccn.loc.gov/2020005361

ISBNs: 978-1-9753-1030-1 (paperback)
       978-1-9753-1031-8 (ebook)

10 9 8 7 6 5 4 3 2 1

LSC-C

Printed in the United States of America

Yen On
150 West 30th Street, 19th Floor
New York, NY 10001

Visit us at yenpress.com
facebook.com/yenpress
twitter.com/yenpress
yenpress.tumblr.com
instagram.com/yenpress

His Exelia trudged forward through the mud, screeching with every slap of dirt against the machine. Its engine was bright red from overheating. Still, he couldn't afford to move any slower, because he knew the moment his vehicle stopped, he would be gunned down.

Turning around, he spotted four state-of-the-art Exelias in pursuit of him. They were AT3s equipped with high-output engines, a staple of the enemy country.

Exelia was a generic term for a small armored vehicle that was approximately ten feet tall. New models were developed as the war demanded it, and at this point, they far exceeded most other firearms.

The maximum speed of his old M4 unit was thirty miles per hour. But the enemy's new models were far faster, so he knew he had no real chance to shake them off. They covered the distance in a mere ten seconds, then used Bullet Magic to shower him with lead.

Goddammit. Why'd this happen? I thought we cadets would be safe!

The cadets were to be kept safe behind the main forces. That was how it had been explained to them. However—

"Nng!"

The Exelia he was riding in exploded. As he flew through the air, the cadet, Rain, clearly saw his unit's manipulator, Athly, blown to smithereens. She didn't so much as scream when her life ended. And as he was showered with the remains of his comrade, Rain rolled down a cliff, taking further blows from the descent.

Goddammit… Why…? Why did this happen?

Looking down, Rain saw a broken bone from his leg fly off into the distance, and a sharp pain that could only be the herald of death pierced his senses. Still, despite the intense agony, he slowly raised his head.

That's…

He saw something rather ominous. A black Exelia, standing in a mountainous region a mere five hundred feet away. A black Exelia… Black?

No way…

He hurriedly peered through the scope on his gun, but unfortunately, his suspicions were confirmed. That black unit belonged to a very specific enemy commander: Major Beluk. There was no mistaking that greasy face. It was Beluk the Butcher, an infamous warrior of the western country who didn't hesitate to gun down even unarmed civilians and children. It seemed he was the man behind this attack…

"Kh…" Rain groaned and set aside his rifle. Then, after rummaging through his breast pocket, he pulled out a single silver bullet. This peculiar-looking bullet was something he'd picked up earlier. He'd found five of them lying around and decided to take them for no reason in particular, but as luck would have it, they were the only bullets he had left, so he had no choice but to use one.

He's about one thousand three hundred feet out…

Even with Bullet Magic to assist him, taking out such a far-off enemy with a single shot would be quite a feat. But—

I have to kill him. Just him, if nothing else. I'll take out the bastard who killed Athly…

Given the circumstances, Rain knew his chance of survival was slim—which was why he refused to die without at least avenging his fallen comrade.

Rain had a ritual, a prayer of sorts. He would always confirm the time on his pocket watch before firing, hoping to accurately confirm the exact moment he would end his target's life…

The time was exactly 2:00 PM.

All right.

After taking ten-odd seconds to adjust his sights, he pulled the trigger. Shortly after that, a crimson flower sprouted in the distance.

He had done it. And through his scope, he confirmed the sight of Beluk's head bursting. *Got him.* However, just as the thought crossed his mind—

"Ah…"

—the world shifted.

MAY THESE LEADEN BATTLEGROUNDS

LEAVE NO TRACE

Bullet Magic and Ghost Programs

CONTENTS

1.   A BULLET THAT SHIFTS THE WORLD

It took only a moment.

What was the best way to describe the sensation? Like film suddenly being rewound, perhaps?

"Ah..."

The world had changed before his very eyes, leaving him dumbstruck.

"...Huh?"

A sense of confusion overwhelmed Rain.

He was no longer in the midst of a battlefield.

"Hurry up, Rain. It's your turn."

...*What?* Rain's fingers were gripping a hand of cards, and he was sitting down comfortably. As far as he could tell, he was playing a game with his friends.

"What, something wrong, Rain? I said it's your turn."

"My...turn...?" Rain mumbled as he looked around. But the entirely peaceful scene only served to deepen his confusion. There was no mistaking the place. He was in the rear base's courtyard, where Major Beluk had first struck. It was the location that had become hell on earth a mere thirty minutes ago.

Or so it should have been…

"Ah… Aaaaaah, aaaaaaaaah!"

Rain couldn't help but throw away the cards in his hands as he panicked.

"Whoa, what the hell, Rain?!"

"C'mon, you don't get to screw around just 'cause you have a shitty hand!"

His friends complained, making their disdain known. But their reactions could not have mattered less to Rain in that moment.

What is this?! What the hell *is this?! What am I doing here?!*

"G-guys! The enemy! Where's the enemy?!"

Why am I just sitting around playing poker…?!

"Enemy?"

His classmate Orca frowned at him. He was a rather crude, built young man, whose major redeeming quality was that he never lied.

"Why the hell would there be enemies around here? We're in the rear, man! The closest thing I've got to an enemy right now is you!"

"Sleepwalk and daydream all you want, but you better pay up!"

His friends complained again, but Rain still couldn't accept the situation.

"…A dream? As if! That was *definitely* real!"

He remembered it all too clearly. The attack had started at 1:30 PM, around the time they usually alternated watch. No one had even predicted it, since this was just a standby base for the rear guard.

However, Beluk the Butcher had struck them anyway, sending Rain and his comrades running. After the cadets were scattered, they were hunted like rabbits. But by some stroke of luck, he'd reached a spot that put him in range of Beluk. And despite the tension, his aim hadn't faltered. At exactly 2:00 PM, Rain had sniped Beluk…

Right, the time…

Rain pulled out his pocket watch to confirm the time, but the sight shocked him.

"What the hell...?"

The hands clearly indicated was still 2:00 PM, meaning it hadn't even been a minute since he'd shot Beluk...

"What's with you guys? What're you even arguing about?"

Four female cadets approached the table after hearing the commotion. Just like Rain, they doubled as students and reserve troops. And among them was...

"Athly..."

A girl with chestnut hair that was tied back and amber eyes that felt out of place on a battlefield. A girl whom, a few moments ago, Rain had seen...

"Huh? What's wrong, Rain?"

"I thought you'd been blown to bits..."

"What's gotten into you?!" Athly yelped with shock, dead but now alive.

Athly. Athly Magmet. Rain's classmate from the officers' academy. He was sure he had witnessed her death with his own two eyes, but...

"This is messed up... How are you not dead?!"

"If anyone's messed up here, it's you!"

"Stop it, Orca! Rain's gone off the deep end because you're shaking him down, hasn't he?! I can't believe I got blown to bits over your nonsense!"

Something... Isn't there something? I need proof... Proof that what I experienced really happened—

"Wait, I know...," Rain muttered as he grabbed the rifle beside him. Then, after opening up the chamber, he inspected the ammunition.

Bullet Magic, as its name implied, was a means to imbue ammunition with various effects and properties. It was also currently the most common weapon in modern warfare. And one of its many applications was the "Engraver" spell, Gale, which imprinted the name of the deceased into the shell of the bullet that killed them. It was magic meant to identify who killed whom, and as such, falsifying results was exceedingly difficult. Lucky for Rain, since the shells weren't ejected from the chamber, he found what he was looking for.

"It's there…!"

Sitting in the ejection chamber was evidence of Major Beluk's death. Namely, a shell that had *Beluk O. Koihen* imprinted on it.

…This is it. Proof that everything I experienced actually happened!

Rain had real, definitive proof that he'd claimed Beluk's life!

"Here, take a look at this!"

"At what?"

"I swear, Rain. You're usually so quiet—if you keep shouting out of nowhere, people will think you're crazy."

Get off my case. Wait, forget that…

"See? It's proof I killed Beluk the Butcher," Rain claimed as he presented the shell to his friends. He knew that would be more than enough to convince them. After all, Beluk was a prominent enemy commander. Sure, they may have been students, but they were also reserve soldiers. There was no way they hadn't heard tales of his horrific deeds. However…

"…Yeah, silver bullets aren't exactly common, but I guess you're right."

"Mm-hmm. Though I wouldn't go around showing that thing to just anyone, Rain. It's proof you killed someone."

Their replies made no sense to Rain.

★   ★   ★

"I don't even know who this Beluk person is, though."

He could tell there was not even a hint of falsehood in their words, and he let out a feeble "Huh…?" in response.

"Who's Beluk? Someone from the West?"

No one present knew who he was.

Even after he returned to the East, Rain desperately scoured every source of information he could to look into Beluk, but he couldn't find a single person who knew of him. There was no trace of him having ever existed.

He's gone.

Everything about Beluk had disappeared. It was as if…

It was as if he'd never existed in the first place.

The land of the East was called O'ltmenia; the land of the West, Harborant.

The friction between the two countries had led to the outbreak of the first war a century ago, and the conflict had been ongoing ever since. The root cause of the dispute, which had eventually led to the fourth war, was a major historical arms race.

Exelias, the quadruped, four-wheeled, small armored vehicles, had first been invented one hundred years ago. And thanks to their superior mobility and defenses, they had constantly evolved ever since.

Rushing through the battlefield, crushing all in its path, the Exelia had become the symbol of war, the apex of weapons technology. However, the graimar nuclear alloy that made up the Exelia's tough yet lightweight fuselage could be mined only in extremely specific, limited locations that were unevenly distributed across regions.

That became the justification for the fourth war. An initial conflict over limited resources, in which soldiers fought to pillage enemy stores, soon turned into a greater conflict. And four years after the start of the war, the flames had not dimmed in the least.

"Kinda feels like the means and ends swapped at some point," Orca said. "We're fighting to get our hands on the alloy, which we then use to make Exelias for further conflict, right? But if we weren't at war, we wouldn't even need the alloy, so what are we really fighting for?"

"Orca."

"Yeah?"

"You're *way* smarter than you look."

"That's just your way of saying I look dumb, you little...!"

Athly and Orca bickered in a lively fashion despite the confined space.

Do you have to be so damn loud when I've got important things on my mind?

"...It wasn't a dream, right?" Rain questioned himself as he rolled the silver shell around in his hand. The name etched onto it was the only proof that he hadn't imagined everything.

"Haaah..." Rain heaved a sigh. They were currently on a transfer train. In the end, no one had targeted them during their three-day garrison period, so they had spent the time in relative peace.

The students of Alestra Academy were on their way back from the front lines. Except there weren't enough train cars, so they were loaded into the luggage car as if they were worth no more than the military equipment around them. Rain looked to the side, catching sight of Athly and Orca grappling, as well as the heavily armored Exelia units behind them.

The small armored vehicles called Exelias were tactical surface weapons said to be so expensive that a single unit was worth the sum of three houses. They could traverse any terrain and were powerful enough to cut through dense forests. Those mechanical beasts had become the primary weapons of war, optimized for use alongside a mage's Bullet Magic.

As Rain studied them, Orca called out to him, "Why so serious, Rain? Chill out already."

"I am calm. I've been calm."

"Yeah, no. I'm not giving you a free pass on that when I apparently died horrifically in your delusions," Athly chimed in. She was one of the few female cadets in the academy, a stubborn girl who had volunteered to become an officer despite her family's objections.

She's from a rich family, so I bet her parents bawled their eyes out.

"But I guess it's not outside the realm of possibility..."

"Huh? What?"

"It wouldn't be strange for any of us to get blown to bits, just like in your daydreams," Athly said. Then she continued, "The hundred years of balance between the two countries was destroyed a long time ago. We'll lose at this rate. From what I hear, a lot of soldiers have died, so there are less and less people on the front lines. Pretty soon, they'll start rounding up high-ranking students to use."

"Are you...?"

"Totally serious. Who knows, they might even send you two out soon. You've got good grades, after all."

As they spoke idly, O'ltmenia's capital came into view, where the Alestra Academy cadets trained.

★   ★   ★

Bullet Magic. A technique in which mages imbued live rounds with mana to produce special effects. Magic itself was a technique inherited from the distant past. Theory couldn't decipher its mechanisms, but there were clearly hidden principles at work in its operation.

However, over the course of a century of warfare, people had sought a more practical application of magic. The result was the development of technology that laced bullets with magical effects, making Bullet Magic widespread among soldiers.

It was developed for the express purpose of murder. A weapon through and through. And given the state of the world, it was the technology in highest demand.

Obviously, the country desired a place to pass down the knowledge, which made Bullet Magic a compulsory subject at Alestra Academy, an institute established to train military officers. The basics of Bullet Magic were taught there, in a classroom setting, but the students were sent out on missions to master it. And once a student completed three years of training, they were given "gun straps." Or in other words, permission to carry a firearm.

…Seriously, what the hell was that?

Rain Lantz, a third-year student at Alestra Academy, was fiddling with his beloved BB77 as he attempted to put his muddled thoughts in order. In the end, he'd failed to find any further proof that Beluk the Butcher had ever existed.

What happened…?

What had happened on that day? It was surely some bizarre phenomenon, but he had no possible explanation for it.

Why couldn't he find any trace of Beluk's existence? Why did no one remember him? Even after he returned to the peaceful atmosphere of Alestra Academy, the sight of that atrocity lingered freshly in Rain's memory. And every single time he thought of it, his gaze fell to the silver shell.

This silver bullet is the only proof I've got...

Unfortunately, it was a bullet he'd randomly picked up, so he had no way to trace its origin. After Beluk the Butcher had attacked the rear base, Rain had run into the nearby forest with Athly to take cover. And as he'd tried to hide, he'd found five of those bullets. He'd used one only because he'd run out of all his other bullets, but as far as he could tell, the only difference was its color. Could it truly have been the cause?

"Hmm?"

His gaze fell onto a newspaper spread out near him.

"Another defeat."

"Mission to retake the Libra Mountain Region has failed."

"State of the war unfavorable. Estimated loss of 7.8 billion zels in damages this season alone."

"We keep losing..."

The articles were the same as ever. They spoke of how O'ltmenia was slowly giving ground to the western country, Harborant. It had been four whole years since the start of the fourth war, and O'ltmenia was not faring well.

There were two major factors to consider in a modern war. One was Bullet Magic, and the other was the Exelias produced from the graimar nuclear alloy. The countries hadn't displayed any major differences in either category at the outbreak of the war, but over the last few years, the West had placed it bets with heavy investments into Exelia development and had eventually reaped the rewards of its success.

As a result, the West's Exelia technology had jumped far ahead of the East's. And as its new Exelias rampaged through the battlefield, everyone came to realize that the East was...

"Hey, gun nerd."

"I'm no gun nerd."

Orca called out to Rain from the neighboring seat. He'd reached out, probably out of boredom, picked up one of the disassembled parts of Rain's gun, and held it up against the light. Rain felt a chill run down his spine; the silver bullets were sitting right next to the parts.

"...Don't touch it directly—the oil will stick to your fingers."

"Why do you even need to keep your gun maintained?"

Rain moved the silver bullets out of sight. Orca didn't seem to notice and kept turning the part in his hand as he used the light to inspect it.

"It's not like we've seen any action."

Haven't seen any action, huh...? Was that day...really an illusion?

Orca's words brought Rain's doubts to the forefront of his mind once more.

Just then, the bell rang.

"Whoa."

Class was starting, so Rain swiftly put his rifle back together and moved it off to the side.

Oddly enough, the teacher was late.

"What do you think happened?"

"I dunno, but I heard something interesting earlier."

"Oh, what?"

"Seems we're getting a transfer student today."

"Huh?" *A transfer student?*

"This is an officers' academy. We don't even have a student exchange program, doofus!"

"Why're you getting all mad at me...? Ever heard the saying 'Don't shoot the messenger'?" Orca whined, then said, "Apparently it's a girl."

"Oh?"

"Don't get too excited, though. Any chick who'd choose to go to an officers' academy is gonna be as self-centered as Athly."

"I heard that!" Athly, who was at the front of the class, turned around and shouted at Orca.

...You've got better hearing than I give you credit for, Rain thought.

Before their snarling had a chance to develop into an actual scuffle, the classroom door slid open, and two people walked in. One of them was First Lieutenant Wilson, who was in charge of logistics. He doubled as an Alestra Academy instructor and an active company officer. However, he wasn't the one who drew their attention.

"Whoa...," Orca exclaimed. Luckily, Rain had managed to keep his voice down. Though he was certainly just as amazed by the sight.

Wow...

This girl before them was clad in the same uniform as the rest of the female students, but she was utterly...*mystifying*. Her white hair was tied up neatly behind her back, her limbs were so dainty that they seemed ready to snap at the slightest touch, and most striking of all...

She's tiny...

She was so petite. However, there was something about her that made her hard to dismiss as a child...

"Do you think those are real?"

"No way..."

There were *two* rifles strapped to the girl's back. One black, the other white. Those were presumably the girl's weapons. One of them was as white as a polished blade, while the other was as black as the darkest of nights.

Some mages wielded absurdly large rifles in order to help fire their Bullet Magic, but the ones on her back seemed far too large for her to handle. Even a single one of them seemed large enough to strain an average person's back, but she carried two as if they were nothing.

Who is *this girl?*

She clearly wasn't normal. The power in her presence, coupled with her two oversize rifles, was frankly unsettling.

Everyone continued to stare at the girl as she cast her gaze around the classroom. And once she raised her face, Rain could see the color of her eyes. They were a silvery hue, matching that of her hair.

Wait, silver...? A mysterious silver-haired, silver-eyed girl who radiated a suspiciously familiar air. And she had appeared right after Rain had used those silver bullets—

Who is she...?

Eventually, the silver girl parted her lips to speak, only to say:

"I see I've walked into the pigsty of a defeated country."

"......"

The girl's clear voice resounded through the classroom. Her tone sounded somewhat authoritative, making everyone's face go blank with surprise. That word, *pigsty*, seemed to hang in the air. But...

"What a wretched sight," the girl continued. And she wasn't about to let up. "So this is what Alestra Academy, the pride and crown jewel of its country, has been reduced to?"

She sighed in abject disappointment.

"You may only be children, but in a few years, you will become officers. If the people leading the organization are so weak-minded, I can see why this country is hurtling toward defeat."

...Children? The same thought passed through the entire

classroom. The appellation sounded wrong coming from her, since she looked a good deal younger than them.

"Really, things haven't changed at all since back then—"

Bam! A sudden sound rang out as the girl attempted to continue her speech. First Lieutenant Wilson, who'd accompanied her, had punched her square on her cheek.

"Kh…"

The students couldn't keep up with what was happening.

Which made perfect sense, really. A girl with two veritable cannons strapped to her back had walked in, called them all pigs, and earned their instructor's wrath.

"Very interesting introduction, transfer student. But I'd say it was a bit too grim," Wilson said, then continued, "Now listen here, and listen *real* good. Never deride our country in my presence. Are we clear?"

His tone seemed to shake the very ground beneath their feet. That was how Wilson spoke when he was angry.

"Take this as a warning. The moment you stepped foot in this academy, *child*, you became no better than an insect. You will obey your superiors' orders. Act out of turn again and I'll burn off that cheeky tongue of yours."

A chill ran down Rain's spine. First Lieutenant Wilson gave off a gentle first impression, but his true nature could be summed up with one word: *severe*. He didn't hesitate to beat his students and didn't forgive those who reported him to superior officers. He had a soldier's mindset, unlike that of most who graduated from an officers' academy. Due to all those factors, he wasn't very popular among the cadets, but he was still a leading figure in the military.

And yet…

"Oh. Deride, you say?"

The silver girl showed no signs of stopping her tirade. Instead, she continued speaking without so much as touching her bruised cheek.

"Enlighten me, then."

"What?"

"Do you really need me to explain? Fine. Putting aside these cowardly brats—as a company officer, you can try to prove me wrong. Tell me, what parts of this country *don't* call for criticism?"

She was incredibly calm for being in front of dozens of people, and especially for having spent no more than a minute in the classroom. It was as if her entire objective was simply to come and level complaints...

"It's been a century now... For the past hundred years, this country has been on the back foot in terms of both Bullet Magic and Exelia technology. The West is looking ten years ahead, while this country is fixated on calculating how much alloy it can mine, never sparing any effort for research and development that would benefit it in the long run," the girl explained in a sharp tone.

"What are you saying...?" Wilson asked.

"The *extremely* obvious facts," the girl stated plainly. Then she continued her rant by saying, "You really are just a bunch of pigs. The only thing on your mind is eating the fodder in front of your eyes. I must say, even dogs are smarter. At least they have the mind to hide their food."

"You little..."

"What? Are you going to claim you're a dog and not a pig? Prove it, then. Bark. Go on. Let me hear you go *woof*."

Wilson's hand went to his waist...and he pulled out his M7 military pistol. With the grip in an overhand hold, he swung the barrel down on the girl's head to shut her mouth with a blow from a metal object. However—

"...No. You're less than a dog."

The girl...didn't dodge. Wilson had moved to strike her without a hint of hesitation, but she didn't budge an inch. The metal hit her head with a dull *thunk*. It was clearly a severe injury. Blood trickled down from her head...but the girl remained stock-still.

"What the...?"

The girl didn't so much as retreat a single step, and that confused Wilson. Seeing that brief opening, the girl finally moved.

No, she wasn't just moving. She was launching a counterattack. The girl twisted her arms in a smooth motion, snatching the same pistol that had split her head.

"Ah, you little...!"

"Too slow."

The pistol swiftly settled into the girl's hand. Wilson had been taken by surprise, but he soon came to his senses and tried to reclaim his stolen weapon.

"Stay still. You disgust me. I don't want your filthy dust touching me."

"Grr..."

The girl pressed the stolen pistol between Wilson's eyes, threatening him. In seconds, she'd completely disarmed him.

"Use your head instead of your body, why don't you...? Oh yes, I know *all* about you, First Lieutenant Wilson. Two months ago, you commanded retreating forces and led fifty soldiers to their deaths because of your reckless orders, didn't you?"

"...So what?" Wilson responded unflinchingly. Then he claimed, "Soldiers should be proud to die for their country."

"Perhaps. But no one wants to die because of an incompetent commander's orders." The girl's finger settled on the trigger.

"What kind of idiot are you? Do you have any idea what

you're doing?! This is a blatant violation of military regulations…
A felony…!"

And…

"A crime, huh?"

…at that exact moment…

"Well, whatever… I supposed my transfer-student facade ends
here."

…Rain noticed something that no one else had.

That's…!

The girl had pulled out a single piece of ammunition…a *silver*
bullet. Then she'd swiftly exchanged it with the one in the gun,
loading it into the cartridge. Only Rain, who'd been carefully
observing her movements, caught it. It took only a moment, but…

That bullet!

It was the mysterious object Rain had happened upon, and
the one that proved Beluk the Butcher was no mere figment of
his imagination. The very same tool that was clearly intrinsically
linked to whatever phenomenon he had experienced. The girl
somehow possessed the very same thing. And—

"Foolishness is the greatest transgression of all."

"Don't—"

Bang!

The deafening sound of a gunshot cut off First Lieutenant Wilson's words, and blood flew through the air as the bullet drilled
into his skull.

And at that exact moment—

—the world shifted with a thump.

2. GHOST "AIR"

"Aaah—"

Everything went dark, and the scenery shifted as if a curtain had fallen over it.

"What...is this place...?" Rain exclaimed, clearly confused. After a short pause, he cried, "Why am I on the battlefield again?!"

He was riding in an Exelia, hidden between the trees. The view was far too familiar for him not to realize he was on a battlefield. This was the Karval Satellite Base, a midsize base positioned in the Northeast. He'd been dispatched here as a reserve soldier in the past, making this his third time visiting the area.

Though that hardly mattered to Rain, who had been in Alestra Academy mere moments prior.

Yes, he was no longer in the safety of his classroom.

Somehow, he had been transported to the middle of a battlefield. *Again... It happened again!*

"Whoa, Rain, what's wrong? You look out of breath all of a sudden," Athly said to him from the driver's seat of the Exelia. Her voice was thick with concern, which made sense, since her partner had suddenly gone pale.

"…Athly?"

"Huh, what's the matter? You nervous after all?"

"No…"

There's no mistaking it…

Rain realized the truth from the way she was acting. Athly seemed to think he'd been here the whole time.

"Then what is it? You look like shit."

"I don't look like shit!"

But I definitely feel *like it…*, Rain thought as he paused for a moment to take a deep breath.

"No… Um, I mean…" Rain trailed off as he paused once again to gather his thoughts. After a short while, he continued with a simple question: "Say, have we been back to school the last few days?"

"Huh? Of course not," Athly replied. Apparently, they'd been away from school for two whole weeks already.

I think I might be losing it…

Taking out his pocket watch, Rain confirmed the time and date. And just as he'd thought, it was September 9…and the dials indicated that it was around 9:00 AM. That meant it had been mere seconds since that mysterious silver girl had appeared in the classroom and shot Wilson dead.

And that was why he had to ask her the most pressing question on his mind.

"Hey, Athly…"

"What's up?"

"You know First Lieutenant Wilson, right? Our logistics instructor…"

This phenomenon was all too hard to process.

"Who? Our logistics instructor is Second Lieutenant Sari."

★   ★   ★

"Seriously, get your act together!"

Rain had confirmed his suspicions by questioning Athly. The Karval Satellite Base was currently in a state of alert. It was under the East's control, but patrolling soldiers had detected western forces nearby. They could have just been scouts, but there was no definitive proof pointing in either direction, so the students had been sent to help shore up the base's defenses.

Still, no matter how many times he'd heard that story, no matter how many sources he'd checked to verify the facts, he found no indication they had returned to Alestra Academy in recent days. And, of course, no one remembered any bizarre silver girl, either.

"Are there even any regular soldiers left in this base?" Rain asked.

"I think so," Athly replied. Though after a moment, she elaborated by saying, "But for some odd reason, this base is short on hands."

For some reason, huh...? Rain knew exactly why. It was because First Lieutenant Wilson and his company had previously been stationed at this base, which meant that his disappearance had left a void.

So Wilson really is gone...

He had disappeared along with all his achievements.

Goddammit, this is messing me up!

The world had shifted a second time. Rain had been thrown onto the battlefield once again, and he was trying to get a grasp on the situation. However, the world wasn't so kind as to indulge him...

"Kh..."

A cannon roared in the distance with a sound characteristic of

Bullet Magic. Dust and fire dispersed in the air, and despite the distance of the blast, the air around them became heavy with tension. All the soldiers in the Exelias started their engines, which roared into action.

"We will now allot tags to the cadets."

A message from a senior officer arrived through the comms.

"You will be given individual orders via intercom! This is live combat, not a test run nor a trial. And as such, you will be treated as a combat unit. Fight to the best of your abilities!"

Code 44. That was the tag allotted to Rain and Athly. Unlike an infantry division, an armored unit of Exelias consisted of several pairs of soldiers. Each pair contained a single manipulator, whose main responsibility was to drive the Exelia, and a gunner, who was in charge of Bullet Magic. Together, they formed the smallest tactical unit on the battlefield. In other words, they formed a partnership in which both individuals shared the same fate. The death of one spelled the demise of the other.

"Codes 7 through 25, move to A3."

"They're in the forest! Widen the line of fire!"

Instructions came through one after another.

"Rain!" Athly cried out to warn him. "They're coming, ten o'clock!"

As soon as she said that, Athly switched gears, turning the vehicle around. A metallic groan resounded as the Exelia activated, sliding rapidly across the terrain on all fours.

The next moment, a form of Bullet Magic called Voldora, or the "Bluefire" spell, burst out from behind them. This particular

Bullet Magic produced massive shock waves and unleashed unique blue-colored flames, covering everything with ash as it tore the ground apart. And from behind that pillar of flames—

"Shit!"

An enemy AT3 suddenly appeared.

"Tch, hang on tight!" Athly shouted as she stomped on the rear pedal to evade, resulting in a sudden brake. The enemy's bullet whizzed past them at paper-thin margins.

"Shoot them down, Rain!"

"I'm on it!"

This was a battle between mages, so the only choice was to counterattack with Bullet Magic. Normal firearms weren't all that effective against mages, meaning the only real choice was to fight fire with fire.

There's no chance of us shaking them off, so we have to take them out here.

Hiding in the flames, the enemy swiftly turned to circle around behind them. They were strong. That much was obvious to Rain from how they were moving. Exelia combat began and ended with manipulators predicting each other's movements.

Those endowed with magical power, regardless of how much of it they had, possessed an ability called Qualia. In simple terms, Qualia was a sixth sense of sorts, an ability to observe the future, which worked most effectively during life-and-death situations. It was this ability that enabled mages to evade bullets moving at supersonic speeds.

Even dozens of soldiers armed with heavy firearms would fail to serve as a distraction against a single mage. Their superior future sight allowed them to evade any ordinary weapon's line of fire without fail. So a battle between mages was a battle between individuals capable of reading the future, which was why the mage who could see further forward came out on top. In other words, a battle of mages depended on who could position their Exelia better.

I see.

Two seconds.

That was all the time it took for their enemy to cut through the conflagration and get in position, aiming to burn them down the moment they stopped to reload. The new model AT3s easily outstripped older Exelias, forcing them into an unfavorable position in the blink of an eye.

Three seconds.

The enemy gunner would be sure of his victory. He likely believed there was no way for them to retaliate in their older machine.

However—

"Sorry, but..."

The next moment...the enemy soldiers were the ones who burst into flames.

"Wha—?" one of them cried out in confusion as the massive blow hit them. They couldn't comprehend what had happened... and it was hard to blame them.

After all, the bullet had flown in from *behind them.*

"This is the end, then," Rain said. "Good-bye," he added frivolously as he pulled the trigger and activated his magic.

As the enemy soldiers stood there, still dumbfounded, Rain fired bullets laced with the Illuminal Bullet Magic, also called the "Void Splitter," a spell that could penetrate even steel plates, and they crashed through their driver's seat windshield and pierced their hearts.

The enemy AT3 stalled with a screech. The shells rolling at Rain's feet had the names of those two soldiers carved onto them.

The Bullet Magic Rain Lantz had employed was called Pharel, or the "Phantasmal Bullet."

"Figures the enemy wouldn't see it coming," he claimed.

"No one would imagine a bullet would *rebound* on them. I mean, a spell that deflects and rebounds bullets? Come on!"

"...When you put it like that, it sounds dumb."

"That's because *it is* dumb," Athly proclaimed. Then she continued to speak, pointing out how no one used it. "Any mage can use the Phantasmal Bullet spell, but no one tries to use it in real combat, because it puts the user in danger of getting hit by the bullet. I think most mages just shoot it off for fun a few times, and that's it."

If one were to examine Pharel purely on its mechanics, it looked fairly straightforward. All it did was make bullets rebound. And that simplicity was why it was one of the first things taught to students at Alestra Academy, alongside how to clean their guns.

Logically, a bullet randomly flicking around the battlefield at supersonic speed was little more than a lethal, dangerous bomb waiting to explode. Predicting its trajectory was too complex, which was why no one tried to make practical use of it.

Still, the fact that it was hard to use meant that so long as it could be controlled, it could become a secret weapon against other mages.

"I'm surprised you can actually make use of it. I'd never be able to pull it off. Is there some trick to reading the trajectory correctly? I've never seen you miss."

"Well, yeah, there *is* a trick to it. But if it was something I could put into words, everyone would be using it."

"...Figures."

The outcome of an Exelia battle was dictated by Qualia. One needed to calculate multiple factors, from information on the enemy, to their surroundings, all the way down to the details of the strategy itself. A good mage needed to piece all of those together individually with their Qualia and base their decisions off the result.

And obviously, one of the most important factors to take into account was the trajectory of bullets, since a mage could use that to avoid enemy attacks. That meant Rain's trick was rather simple. He simply used Pharel to make bullets whiz about. But when combined with future sight strong enough to predict such complicated patterns...it became a weapon with lethal accuracy.

"Code 44 to HQ. One enemy Exelia eliminated at point B2," Athly reported.

"Good job. Satisfying results for cadets on a real battlefield. But there are still many enemies left. Change of orders: Code 44 is to proceed to point C1 and join the front line." The response came promptly. And with that, the transmission cut off.

"...Maybe I should've waited a bit before reporting our success."

"Agreed."

Unfortunately, it was too late to change their minds. And as such, Athly accelerated the Exelia toward the designated point to offer assistance to their allies. However—

"Ugh..."

When they reached point C1, all they found were corpses.

"How many people is this...?"

"...Don't count. Just confirm the status of their rigs."

Five allied Exelias had defended this position...and all of them were now scrap. Their thick armor had been peeled away, and the characteristic high-speed legs were bent to the point that discerning their original shape was difficult. The wreckage was smoldering, and the multiple machine guns employed for defense had been destroyed. Only the remains were left to mark the overwhelming loss.

"Shit..."

The enemy has...ten units? Bullshit! Maybe three times that number would explain this.

Right as that crossed Rain's mind...

"Huh?"

...it happened.

"Who's that...?" Athly asked in confusion. And perfectly understandable confusion at that, because a lone girl was walking over the remains and corpses.

It's...

No, not just any girl. A lone *silver* girl with two oversize rifles on her back.

It's her...!

It was the girl on the forefront of Rain's mind, the one who'd shot Wilson in the classroom.

What is she doing here...?!

All he could think of in that moment was the silver bullet, as well as the unfamiliar, unknown girl who possessed it.

"...Wait here, Athly. If any enemies appear, I'll drop everything and come back, understand?"

"Ah, wait—!"

Not sparing an ear for Athly's attempts to stop him, Rain disembarked from the Exelia, which drew the girl's attention.

The girl simply watched Rain as he approached her, then she gently hopped off the Exelias' wreckage, landing with an awfully soft thud. The sound was so light that it seemed the firearms she was carrying carried no weight at all…as if everything about her was made of air. As if she wasn't even human.

There was only a short thirty-foot gap between them. And at her back, along with her two cannons, Rain spotted the moonlit night sky.

"Don't move," he barked as he pulled out his pistol and aimed it at the girl. After a short pause, he asked, "Who are you?"

"…Why the sudden questions?"

"Answer me!"

"…Pipe down, child," the girl chided him without sparing him a single glance, then continued, "It's such a still, soothing night. The wind has finally died down, but I keep hearing crackling coming from all over the place. Such a racket… Can't you children fight a little more quietly?"

"Answer me. Who are you?"

"What is your problem? Why are you so…upset?"

She wasn't giving him the time of day.

…No choice, then.

"The silver bullet."

"Oh my…"

Silver… The moment he said that word, the girl's expression changed.

"May as well lay all my cards out on the table, I guess…," he said. "I'm a student of Alestra Academy who still remembers First Lieutenant Wilson. I know he still existed earlier today, so

I checked to see if anyone else remembered him. But everyone I asked said they'd never heard of him and acted like I was crazy. I could tell they weren't lying, but I won't let you say you don't remember him."

This silver girl's presence felt faint, as if she might disappear at any moment along with the flickering pale flames. But Rain didn't let up, since he knew it was her. He knew that she was the one who had murdered Wilson.

"I saw it. I saw the silver bullet you loaded into his gun before you shot him."

With his pistol's muzzle still fixed on her, Rain reached into his breast pocket, pulled out something he'd kept hidden inside it, and presented it to the girl. It was a bullet's shell that proved Rain had killed Beluk the Butcher. A dull gray shell that yet shined with an uncanny luster.

It was clearly the source of all the strange phenomena around Rain. The name on this bullet was the only remaining evidence that the man had ever existed. And so, with that bullet in hand, he asked the burning questions on his mind: "Answer me. What *the hell* is this bullet? Why do people shot with one disappear without a trace?"

How long did that silence last? It was honestly hard to tell. Eventually, however, after acting as if she was pondering all the while...

"Oh, I see. So it's you..."

...the girl...

"You're the one who picked me up."

...said something completely incomprehensible.

Picked...me up?

"Kh...!"

Those words sent shivers down Rain's spine.

"Well, you look a bit weak, but so be it. Say, what's your na— Whoa!"

Before she could finish her sentence, Rain fired a single bullet at the girl's feet.

"What's the big idea?!"

"I'm the one asking questions here. Answer me. Who are you?"

"…Children these days are quite impatient."

Who're you calling a child…? You're definitely younger than I am!

"Petite" was the perfect way to describe her. It was easy to forget her short stature before her powerful sense of pressure, the massive rifles on her back, and her mysterious silver eyes, but it was still impossible to deny.

"Hey, stop talking about children, and just answer the damn question."

"Air."

"Huh?"

"I am a Ghost, Air."

"Ghost?"

The hell does that mean?

"And I am likely the one with the answers you seek. I can tell you all about the bullet you're holding, of course, and so much more."

"In that case—"

"I gave you my name, but you haven't given me yours. Haven't you heard of manners? If you don't tell me your name, I won't know what to call you." Air interrupted Rain to chastise his lack of courtesy. Though given the situation, manners were the last thing on his mind.

"I'm Rain. Rain Lantz."

"And your affiliation?"

"Third-year student at Alestra Academy. Currently Code 44 of the cadet corps."

"Code 44. I see."

And just as the girl said, "A fine number," it happened.

"Rain, get back! Hurry!" Athly cried out to him. And at that exact moment, an inferno exploded out from behind them.

"Wha—?"

His field of vision turned red as a deluge of flames rushed by his face.

Damn, it's hot...

It was a long-distance bombardment from the enemy.

"Ugh..."

"Athly!"

The sight of her broken body from the other day flashed before his eyes. But this time, luck was on her side. The bombardment missed its mark, and she avoided a direct hit. But unfortunately, her body jolted violently in the driver's seat, and she fell limp. The attack had knocked her out.

"...Kh!"

This was an *extremely* dangerous situation.

What the hell do I do? Rain thought. He couldn't drive the Exelia on his own. Sure, he could at least move the machine, but it was an armored vehicle that only select elites could drive. Proper use required a great deal of training, so any actual combat measures were impossible on his own. Still, he didn't have the time to second-guess himself. He could already see the enemy Exelias approaching.

Dammit...

He was out of time. So Rain picked up Athly's limp body and

moved it to the back, vacating the driver's seat. He had no choice but to take the wheel.

If I'm going to die either way, I should at least—

"Up we go."

Right when he started steeling his resolve, someone hopped into the driver's seat instead.

"...Huh?"

"My word, you're helpless."

It was the silver girl, Air. She straddled the Exelia's driver seat as if it was the most natural thing in the world and said, "Let's move."

Rain didn't even have time to object. Within a moment, a jolt swung his body.

Wha—?!

The Exelia groaned as if it was tearing itself out of the ground, then suddenly began accelerating. The next moment, it braked hard enough to blur their surroundings, and the wheels dug into the ground, moving them forward with a slide.

"Whoa, whoaaaaaa!"

"Keep your mouth shut. You'll bite your tongue," Air stated as she adjusted her course to avoid a tree. The vehicle continuously creaked as she rapidly switched gears. Exelias had steering wheels, so simple movements didn't require extensive training. However, the most unique aspect of the Exelia was the mobility granted by its nature as a quadruped vehicle whose four wheels could each be moved independently. It was the same as operating four unicycles as once.

That was what set it apart from other vehicles. It wasn't a single unit unified by brakes, a clutch, and gears. Each of its four legs had to be controlled manually to allow for the overwhelming mobility that gave the Exelia its value.

Of course, that required an innate disposition for the task and rigorous training. Even Athly, who had often been praised for her natural talent, needed six months before she could make any sharp turns. And yet...

"Wait, how...? How are you doing this?!"

The silver girl's skills were impeccable. While maintaining peak speed, she cruised through the dark forest. Switching gears nimbly, she controlled the wheels as if they were her limbs, and she whizzed past the trees as if she were the wind itself.

Who the hell is she...?!

Air was an unfamiliar girl who called herself a Ghost, which was odd enough, but Rain doubted there was anyone in the army who could handle an Exelia as well as she could. She was like a war hero who had lived through countless battlefields. Frankly, the sight was so incredible that Rain was in awe.

"Who the hell are you...?"

"Didn't you hear me? I'm a Ghost."

"That's not what I mean!"

"Chatting is fun and all, but could you at least fire a few warning shots?"

At her advice, Rain noticed two enemy units in hot pursuit of them. Air's driving may have been perfect, but the difference in machine specs was all too real. It was as unfair as an adult joining in on a children's game of tag. And that unfairness allowed the enemy units to make up for the gap in their piloting skills.

Warning shots...? No way, their machines are far better than ours...

Rain's hands shivered as they gripped his gun. It seemed his ability to think clearly had faltered in the face of encroaching death. However, her composed voice broke him out of his despair and into action.

"...Hmph. Shaking them off will prove to be difficult, it seems. Well, I suppose this is about as much as I'd expect from this bucket of bolts...," Air said in a nonchalant manner and then added, "...and a child."

"Where do you get off calling me a child?"

"I'm going to make a turn soon. Get your next Bullet Magic ready."

"What?"

"If we can't shake them off, our only option is to fight them."

The Exelia lurched forward. Her driving was just as perfect as earlier, but the enemy was still closing the distance.

"I'll turn the rig around and dive straight at the enemy. At that point, they'll be straight ahead of us. There are four enemies across the two units, but I want you to aim at the gunner in the unit to the right. Match your timing with mine." Air barked her orders at Rain. And a moment later, she added, "Oh, and the bullet you'll be using is the Devil's Bullet."

Devil's Bullet...?

"That silver bullet you have. That's what it's called," she explained. "Normally, it's a special bullet only I can produce, but you had the misfortune of finding some. Make sure you don't miss."

As soon as she finished explaining her plan, Air flipped the Exelia around. She used a tree as a spring to do a one-eighty, then rushed toward the approaching enemies.

Holy shit, this lunatic...

There was no turning back, no other chance of survival, which meant Rain had no real choice in the matter.

Oh, to hell with this…!

He loaded the silver bullet, the *Devil's Bullet*, into his rifle.

I have to make this shot…!

The enemy reacted swiftly, firing off one Bullet Magic after another. Air avoided a lethal bullet by the skin of her teeth, and then another, leaving the ammunition to burst behind them. The enemy had been so close to hitting them that Rain almost believed Air had dodged by accident.

The next moment, Rain focused his Qualia. It felt as if time had ground to a halt… They were 140 feet away from the enemy as he picked up the enemy's visage through the scope on his rifle.

It was dark out. Only scant moonlight shined down. But he could still see the one he was looking for illuminated by the raging flames.

There he is…

Rain saw the face of the gunner peeking out from behind the windshield. So he acted according to Air's instructions. He couldn't make any sense of the situation, so his best option was to take out the gunner.

Out of habit, he examined his pocket watch. The time was 7:15 PM.

Eat this! he thought as he squeezed the trigger. Suddenly, a whiff of gunpowder filled his nostrils, and recoil ran through his entire body, starting at his index finger. The bullet he'd fired didn't miss its mark. It exceeded the opponent's Qualia and lodged itself straight in the enemy gunner's abdomen.

He couldn't see the spray of red blood in the darkness, but he could still tell.

He died instantly.

Air braked at the perfect moment, which ended up augmenting Rain's shot. Like a puppet with its strings cut, the enemy tumbled off the vehicle, hitting the ground and soaking it with blood.

That was when *it* happened.

"Well done."

As the silver girl's voice echoed around him…

"Ugh…"

…the world swirled and shifted.

And everything faded to black.

"_____"

The phenomenon wasn't as extreme as the previous times. The change hadn't transported him to an entirely new location. All he'd felt was a swirling sensation of motion.

"…Ah."

"Oh, you noticed?"

"This is…"

"Looks like the battle's over for now."

Rain jolted awake, apparently having been seated against a tree in the forest. And right next to him was…

"Athly…!"

"It's fine—she's just asleep."

Like Air said, his partner was sleeping on top of a tree stump. She was unharmed, simply resting due to exhaustion. Nothing seemed off about her.

…I need to calm down and get a handle on the situation.

Checking his pocket watch, he noticed it was 7:15 PM. Less than a minute since he'd shot an enemy gunner who'd been chasing them.

There was no mistaking it. It had happened again.

This is nuts...

Their Exelia was parked beside them. And there, sitting on top of the fuselage, was a silver girl with two large rifles strapped to her back.

"We seem to be pretty far from the front lines," Air commented. "Well, I suppose everything went as planned." The girl looked around cheerfully. "Normally, you'd probably contact the East's headquarters in this situation, but I've never been one for plunging headlong into anything, and waiting until we receive further instructions is... Ah!"

"All eastern forces, incoming orders."

And that was because she was surprised by the orders flowing out through the radio.

"Our enemies are retreating. Victory is ours. However, some details about the situation are still unclear. Codes 3 to 21 are to remain on the front lines. All cadets are to conclude hostilities and return to base."

—Our enemies are retreating.

—Victory.

—All cadets are to conclude hostilities.

It seemed the battle was drawing to a close. The night raid had concluded.

Did I...end it?

The world had shifted...

This is absurd...

"Really? That's so boring." Air seemed upset upon hearing the order to retreat. "I knew I picked the right person to erase, but it feels rather dull when things go this well. Is the West's condition so shaky that removing one unit is enough to turn the tide? Or are they just a cautious bunch? I wonder what the point of this operation even was... Something feels off."

The silver girl was whispering to herself, but Rain picked up that she was saying she'd engineered this whole situation. That made perfect sense, as she was the one who'd picked Rain's target earlier.

"Ugh, what the hell is going on?! You..."

"Hmm?"

"Who the hell are you...? None of this makes any sense!"

"Seriously, you're still asking me that? How many times do I have to tell you?" Air replied as the night wind moved through her lovely silver locks. "I am Air, a Ghost."

Ghost...

"And I'm also the rightful owner of the Devil's Bullet you possess."

The Devil's Bullet...

"What do you mean by 'Ghost,' exactly?"

"A dead person."

Rain knew that much already. The word *ghost* was rather common, after all. But he couldn't understand why the girl described herself as one.

Was she saying she was the spirit of a person who had passed away? That description didn't fit the girl in front of him, as she seemed all too corporeal. Air stood on top of the Exelia, forcing Rain to look up at her, but no matter how hard he looked, he didn't find any hint of her being dead or transparent.

"What, are you trying to say...you're not human?"

"Well, I'm not sure what your definition of *human* is, but I've still got my legs."

"Your legs?"

"Isn't that what they say in the West? That the dead don't have legs."

"Huh?"

"See?" Air said as she rolled up her skirt.

"Mgh!"

"Ha-ha-ha-ha! What's with you? I know you're a cadet, but you're still a soldier. I didn't think you'd be this demure!" Air chuckled teasingly. She was laughing at his expense.

"Quit messing with me!"

"I must say, that blush on your cheeks isn't very intimidating."

The girl looked down on him as she switched from outright laughter to a smug smirk. That haughty attitude didn't really fit her girlish appearance, but she seemed to have a mean streak all the same.

This little...!

She had an elusive air about her, and her appearance felt removed from reality. Instead of a child's innocence, she carried a sense of unperturbed composure that stemmed from accumulated experience.

And she definitely had more life experience than him...a fact that was made all too clear by how Rain had reacted to her rolling up her skirt.

"Don't look down on me, dammit!" Rain exclaimed as he raised his gaze back to the girl.

"Have another," Air said as she flashed him a second time, flipping up her skirt.

"Gah!"

This time, Rain got a clear glimpse of her panties.

"Ha-ha-ha-ha! Did you hear yourself?! You actually went 'Gah'! Who even makes those kinds of noises?! Ha-ha-ha!"

"...I told you to quit messing with me! Look, I'm trying to have a serious conversation with you."

"Please. If you're that wet behind the ears, then you're the one who's not taking things seriously," the girl claimed as her cheer was replace by a much more intense glare.

Ugh...

A chill ran through Rain, and he felt goose bumps on his skin. It was an ominous warning that this girl, Air, was far from ordinary. And upon seeing Rain's reaction, she exhaled audibly.

"Let me ask just in case, then. Do you know anything about the war between the East and the West from one hundred years ago?"

"Huh?"

Why's she asking that?

"One hundred years ago... You mean the first war?"

"Yes, that one."

Her tone implied that she didn't expect anyone to remember what had happened. It was the source of the current conflict, so the events that had transpired were taught in history classes. However, since political affairs and weaponry were so different back then, his teachers never went into too much detail.

One hundred years ago...

"How would I know exactly what happened?"

"It seems the children of this age are far more illiterate than I thought."

"This again...?"

Who're you calling a child? You're definitely younger than I am, you stubborn brat! Rain thought, overcome by his anger.

"Well, no matter. Let's put that aside for now. The important thing here isn't me, but this," Air said as she reached into her breast pocket and pulled out a silver bullet.

"The Devil's Bullet…"

"Right. This bullet has my own personal Bullet Magic sealed into it. It's called the Devil's Bullet."

The light reflected off its lustrous surface, much like it would have with silverware.

"And since you've used it more than once already, you probably already know what it does. You may be rather dense, but as they say, the third time's the charm. Don't disappoint me, now. This is a test."

Rain didn't understand how or why she was testing him, but he intended to answer anyway. In the end, all he could do was form an opinion based on his experiences.

The first time, Rain had shot Beluk the Butcher with a silver bullet, and the world had shifted. The second time, Air had shot First Lieutenant Wilson in the classroom, and the world had shifted again. The third time, Rain had shot the gunner in an enemy Exelia, and the outcome of the battle had changed, concluding the enemy raid.

He'd already considered the possibility, but common sense had kept urging him to discard the notion. But by now, he'd been convinced.

"This bullet…," Rain said, ready to explain the Devil's Bullet's world-changing powers.

"This bullet deletes the very existence of those it kills."

After a short pause…

"Correct," Air finally replied. "Though to be more precise,

it erases everything relating to whoever it kills from this world. That is the power the Devil's Bullet holds."

Her explanation sounded rather ridiculous, but Rain didn't feel the need to cut her off.

"This is my unique form of Bullet Magic. No one else can use it, and even if someone managed to reproduce the methods behind it, no one would be able to activate it. It's my very own personal brand of Bullet Magic."

The Devil's Bullet... A magical bullet that erased a person's existence.

"That explains it..."

They disappeared from everyone's memories.

"It does more than just erase its victims from everyone else's memories and records, though. It also undoes everything they've achieved in their lives, rendering all their accomplishments null and void. So if, for example, you were to shoot the inventor of the automobile with this bullet, the ensuing world would not have cars, as they had never been created. And if Person B killed Person A, and you shot B with this bullet...the world would shift to one where A survived."

The Devil's Bullet eradicated the very existence of anyone it hit, shifting the world into one where that person never even existed.

"The shift to a world without that person is known as 'Reprogramming.'"

"Reprogramming..."

That was the name of the phenomenon that shifted the foundations of the world.

"Well, this will have to do for tonight," Air stated as she turned around and started walking away.

"Hey, where are you going?"

"Back. For today, at least. I've completed my objective."

"Your objective?"

"Finding you."

Once again, she said something that made no sense.

Finding...me?

"I transferred into Alestra Academy for that purpose. Though I *did* want to get rid of that useless officer while I was at it. Originally, hundreds would've died in vain here because Wilson prolonged the battle for no reason, but now it's peaceful."

The girl walked away, praising herself on a job well done. However, Rain did not intend to just let her go on her merry way. She still hadn't explained everything that had happened to him thus far.

Rain set off after the retreating girl, jogging to catch up. Thankfully, she was walking at a leisurely pace, so he closed the gap within ten seconds. But right when he reached out to grab her shoulder...

"Ah!" screamed Rain as his body was lifted off the ground and flung back down.

"Ugh, that hurts!"

"Don't touch me," Air muttered in a voice cold enough to freeze the blood in Rain's veins. "I may be a Ghost, but I have the same flesh as you. I get tired after running; I can sweat, and I can die of starvation. But that does not give you the right to lay your hands on me."

—Don't touch me.

—I have nothing in common with a human like you.

Rain could immediately tell he had been rejected.

What...?

However, he was also sensing a kind of dissonance.

Where the hell did that come from...?

Her reaction seemed unnatural. Sure, Air had always treated human lives flippantly and referred to most people as fools. But this? It felt excessive. Though in a way, it was the first truly human reaction Rain had seen from her.

Something's...

Something was wrong. She had to have a specific reason she hated people touching her.

"Whatever, it's fine."

Before Rain could dwell on the matter, Air dispelled the tension.

"We'll meet again soon enough. Until we do, keep training your Bullet Magic and get used to combat."

"Wait, I still have some questions."

"Oh, and get used to being around girls, too."

"......"

"I hope the next time we meet, you'll be mature enough to not go red at the sight of a girl's panties. All right, Rain Lunch?"

With that teasing farewell, Air walked off into the forest, and silence settled over the area once more. Even the sound of the wind felt fainter than before.

"...Who're you calling Lunch?"

I'm not your damn food. It's Lantz, dammit! Rain Lantz!

"...Ah, shit."

Now alone, Rain could only look inward to make sense of what she'd told him.

A Ghost. The Devil's Bullet. Bullet Magic that erases people's existence and shifts the fabric of the world...

"What the hell?"

Five minutes later, Athly woke up, and they made their way back to base.

The incessant downpour grew stronger.

The silver girl had fled long and desperately, but she'd eventually been captured when her stamina expired.

I curse you all!

She thrashed and struggled, but the cold barrel of a gun poked against her back.

I curse you all! May you all rot and fester—

Her heart had been consumed by grudges and malice. That black, despicable, all-too-stagnant emotion was...

"No— Wait, stop, noooooo!"

She screamed. But unfortunately, the executioner showed no mercy. He pulled the trigger and pierced her heart, splashing fresh blood across the virgin snow.

The time was 2:36 PM. The battle over the East's Ental Mountain Range had ended earlier in a resounding victory for the defending side. The enemy had announced they were forfeiting at 2:00 AM and bitterly handed over control of the entire region.

The casualties came out to five Exelias for the East and thirty from the West, so it wasn't at all surprising that the West had retreated. Losing an entire company's worth of units was a massive blow. And additionally, one of the West's officers had been captured.

Hmm, who was that again? Oh, right. Commodore Wood.

High-ranking officers didn't often take direct command of the battlefield, but Commodore Wood was known as a strict, seasoned veteran who'd never lost a battle. In fact, he'd caused so much trouble for the East over the years that he'd earned the moniker "Speedy Devil."

But that venerated soldier had been reduced to the state of a common criminal, chained hand and foot. Someone had likely already punched him, as his face was red and swollen. From an outsider's perspective, he was just a powerless old man. Even an experienced man of valor could be reduced to this.

"Man, even the Speedy Devil looks like any old fart without his fancy getup."

"Show him a little respect," Rain said as he cast a sidelong glance at Orca. "Commodore Wood's a well-known soldier, even if he is our enemy. We shouldn't make light of him."

"I know, but…"

The East's cadets had returned to base unharmed. And Orca, who seemed to be in perfect shape, seemed particularly lax. "I hear you, but you've gotta admit that he made a pretty big mistake today."

"A mistake, huh?"

"I mean, look at how bad we crushed them. How else would you describe it?"

"Yeah, good point…"

"Well, thanks to that, we got away with basically zero losses, so I ain't complaining! Ha-ha-ha!"

The cadets had been dispatched in five units, made up of ten members in total. None of them were exhausted, though, because their victory had been overwhelming. The battle had ended in an exceedingly favorable position for the East... An almost too favorable position, in fact.

"...Sorry, Orca, I'm going to step outside."

"Something wrong? We're gonna celebrate while we wait for further orders. Don't ditch us already."

"I wouldn't celebrate now if I were you."

"Still, you sure you're fine? You said you were feeling kinda sick the other day, too."

"...I'm fine. Just need a little rest," Rain said as he left his classmates behind, heading for the tent in the rear of the base. It was a designated sleeping area, so there was no one around.

It's done... I got away with it again.

Rain lowered his beloved TK rifle, which wasn't formally used by the military. Then he lifted the slide, and the firing chamber opened with a loud click. A puff of gunpowder hissed into the air as ten or so shells rolled out of the rifle...

"......"

And each one had the name of a human being etched onto it.

He'd gunned down ten people, using a silver bullet on each.

"I see you're making good use of it." A mysterious voice suddenly praised him, and Rain wheeled around with a start. He'd made sure he was alone, but...

"You..."

"Been a while, hasn't it?" The silver girl had appeared out of thin air. "I see you've been working hard."

"...I wouldn't exactly say that."

"Oh, come now. It's important to at least maintain the facade with pleasantries."

Air approached him, mouthing a *Now then* before Rain could even react. And as soon as she got within arm's reach of him, she snatched the pouch dangling from his belt.

"Wait, give it back!"

"No."

Rain reached out to grab it, but he wasn't fast enough.

"I gave you a trial period, so it's only fair I grade you now, right?"

Air poured the contents of the pouch onto the ground. She knew there were a lot in there based on its weight, but when she saw the sheer number of objects spilling out...

"Ha...ha-ha-ha!"

There were well over two hundred shells...and they were all silver.

"Ha-ha-ha-ha-ha-ha-ha-ha-ha-ha-ha-ha-ha-ha!"

There was only one type of ammo that used those specific silver casings: the Devil's Bullet. Scattered over the floor were the remains of those bullets, which served as the only tangible proof of the hundreds of human beings who'd been wiped from existence.

"I must say, I'm impressed. I didn't think you'd have a field day with them! Ha-ha-ha-ha! I've never met such a trigger-happy fool before!" Air laughed loudly upon catching sight of Rain's possessions. Hundreds of shells were spread out on the ground.

"Let's count, then... Oh, two hundred four. Well, aren't you an eager beaver? It's only been ten days, yet you've accomplished so much." Air smirked at him. Rain hated her flippancy about this, but he could not deny them.

"Could you stop laughing already?"

"I suppose I should. I've laughed enough for all the people you've killed already."

Ten days. That was how long it'd been since he'd found those first five bullets. And as long as he had those shells in hand, he could freely produce more.

"Why did you come now?"

"Oh, there's no deep reason behind it. I decided it was best to gather more information about this world, so I buckled down to work in the grand library. And then I saw this article in the newspaper this morning."

Air tossed a newspaper at Rain. It had the following headline:

The eastern nation, O'ltmenia, is taking charge.
Four eastern territories reclaimed.

"This is the first time I've seen one fool change the country so much...change the very course of *history*."

"You don't have to call me a fool."

"Oh, but you certainly are one. Don't you think you went too far?"

Only the two of them knew what had happened, but things had definitely changed. In just ten days, every aspect of the conflict between the East and the West had shifted.

Ever since the war began four years ago, the East had been on the back foot. But starting ten days ago, it had experienced a sudden change of fortune.

"I knew you were doing quite a bit, but still."

The East's position continued to improve. It had won local battles in quick succession, reclaimed four territories, and repeatedly broken through the West's once unbreakable defensive line, wiping away the cloud of defeat.

How could the situation have changed so drastically when no new technology or strategies had been introduced? Many scholars and generals sought the answer to that question, but they were left with only theories.

None of them knew the truth. None of them even had a chance of discovering the truth. No one would've guessed that a single boy, with bullets laced with mysterious magic, was responsible.

"You erased fifty people over the past three days, right?" Air asked as she arranged the silver shells of the Devil's Bullets in a meaningless formation. "You really let loose. More than I thought you would, to be honest. It breaks most people—either that or they go mad from the power and start abusing it, only to die."

Air cast her gaze at Rain, a boy who looked no different from any other cadet. A boy whose only real talent was his ability to make use of ricocheting bullets.

"...What?"

"I was just thinking how interesting your eyes have become."

Rain Lantz's gaze was now akin to that of a ferocious beast—but he'd likely always been like that at heart. Those weren't the eyes of a man drunk on power, but the calm, collected eyes of one who'd mulled over things rationally and chosen to erase the lives of hundreds of officers to seize control of the battlefield.

And in so doing, he'd permanently altered the world in a way that was extremely hard to detect.

No one noticed the truth.

No one noticed the Reprogramming.

Anyone shot by the Devil's Bullet had every trace of their existence removed from the annals of history. The moment they died, the world shifted to one where they'd never even existed.

And so no one could judge him for it.

"Well then, what do you want from me now, Ghost?" Rain asked.

"Nothing much."

"……"

She was getting on his nerves.

"…Ugh, please. You've come to take my life, haven't you?"

"Huh? Me, take your life? Now, why would I ever do that?"

"What do you mean, why…?" Rain mumbled, confused by her words. Then, seeing the look of shock on her face, he added, "I mean…this is the Devil's Bullet, right?"

The devil… Yes, the *Devil's* Bullet. Air had definitely used that word to describe the silver bullet…and the meaning of that term was rather evident.

"Didn't you give me this power as some sort of…I dunno, deal with the devil? In exchange, you claim my soul?"

"Did they drop you on your head when you were born?"

"……"

Just bear with it. Hitting her won't get you anywhere.

"Don't treat me like the biblical devil. I'll have you know that I'm the most state-of-the-art model available. Besides, you said I'd take your soul, but do souls even exist? I can't say I've ever seen one."

"…I mean, same here."

"Right? I can't take something you don't have," Air stated as she furrowed her brow.

"Well, sure, but…"

"I'm glad we've come to an understanding."

…Have we?

"Anyway, your free trial expires today. If you wish to keep using my power, you'll have to make a pact with me."

"See, there *is* a catch."

Some state-of-the-art model you are.

"So, a pact?"

"Right. In exchange for those silver bullets, I desire every-thing that you are."

Wow, that's a pretty shitty deal...

The girl demanded his whole self in recompense. And upon hearing her conditions, Rain murmured, "A devil..."

"Right. Ghosts are one kind of devil."

This again...

Air had called herself that repeatedly, and over the last ten days, Rain had tried to figure out what she meant, to no avail.

A ghost...

"Ugh, I'm growing tired of this back-and-forth. It's about time I explained things to you properly. I doubt I'll find another gunslinger as trigger-happy as you, so you'll have to do," Air said as her hand moved to draw the white gun on her back.

Ah... Rain reached for his own gun reflexively. Without even thinking, he pulled it out and moved the muzzle toward her. However—

"You're slow," Air stated. With her overwhelming speed, she had shot him before Rain could even target her.

"What...?"

"Let me show you a dream."

And as she said that, her bullet traveled straight into Rain's head, making him lose all strength and crumple to his knees...

Ugh...

A hazy scene played out before his eyes. It was a distorted image, with foggy, undulating edges. However, after a few seconds, the blurry world grew clearer.

Oh, this is…

It was a memory. There was a form of Bullet Magic that allowed one to display their memories—the "Projector" spell, Reluminance. The memories were loaded into a bullet, which was then shot into a person so they could relive them. A most uncommon, rarely used spell.

Rain was on a battlefield. *Whose memory is this…?*

A recollection of a war? Flames raged, screams of pain tore through the sky, and armored vehicles raced forward, trampling the remains of the dead. Old Exelias tore through enemy lines, facing off in the dozens.

And that was when *she* suddenly appeared. A silver girl, smiling pleasantly as she destroyed one enemy after another.

That's… She was a rather beautiful, striking girl. Wielding the cannon on her back, she unleashed Bullet Magic and made quick work of the Exelias. It was as if a Valkyrie had descended onto the battlefield.

The girl's gallant stride made her attractive features all the more radiant. And by crushing the enemy with her own two hands, she'd brought that war to an end.

She'd stopped all the fighting, which made her a hero. However, when the image changed, Rain was dumbstruck.

Huh…?

"Why…? Why?!"

The same silver star of the battlefield was bound in chains like a felon.

"I fought while wagering everything I had…so why?!"

The military tribunal had made its judgment. And its verdict was…capital punishment.

"No— Wait, stop, noooooo!"

The moment she heard about her sentence, the girl flew into a rage. Thanks to some impromptu use of Bullet Magic, she stole a nearby guard's pistol and escaped the place. Unfortunately, her pursuers soon recaptured her.

Lying atop the white snow, the girl wept bitterly. And yet they still shot straight through her heart. They executed her...and the memory cut off there.

"Ugh, aaah!" Rain woke from the vision with a start, his heart beating like a drum. He'd been exposed to those memories for only a few seconds, but his forehead was slick with cold sweat. Also, his consciousness felt unfocused, as if he'd been intoxicated. "That... was..."

"Yes, that's right. Those were my memories," Air declared. "Now allow me to introduce myself once more."

At those words, the girl straightened and looked Rain right in the eye.

"I am a mage who was once affiliated with the First Unit of Harborant's ground forces. And one hundred years ago, I was executed by the military, who sealed my very existence into a bullet and turned me into a Ghost."

A Ghost. Or in other words...

"Then you really did..."

"I died. A long time ago..."

Her voice was perfectly detached as she spoke of her own demise.

"It happened just like in the memory I showed you. They shot me through the heart. And time after time, people like you picked me up, which was how I retained my consciousness for so long. Though I've been dormant the past twenty years," Air added.

There was no melancholy in her voice, no resentment or malice. It honestly almost sounded as if she didn't care about anything she was saying.

"Oh, allow me to correct myself. My real name is Air Arland Noah. I'm a mage who was given an unprecedented promotion at the age of fourteen. As a commander, I led a five-day defensive line to victory during the concluding battle of the first war in 1881. And I was once a dyed-in-the-wool, true-blue war hero who saved her country."

Rain couldn't laugh off her words. After all, he'd just seen her memories. That battlefield had been full of first-generation Exelias, which were clearly from a century ago. Plus, he'd seen the girl's incredible prowess as she danced across that battlefield. However, he'd also seen the scene that followed...

"An execution..."

"Yes. I was killed."

It was a cruel, ghastly conclusion...

"My own country put me on trial and sent me to the gallows."

"Why...?"

"The battle you saw was the final one of the first war, the Battle of Anval. I led them to victory in that battle, but while I was a mage...I was also a student. The people in charge were scared that having a child war hero would shame them. Not only did they send children who weren't ready for war into battle, but one of them even led them to victory. That fact greatly complicated the country's righteous narrative. That's...the only reason, really."

They'd sentenced her to death for such a simple reason. Which was why, on the verge of death...

"I cursed them."

May you all rot and fester—

That had been her greatest wish. And at the very end, her lingering grudge had been preserved...

"My existence was sealed into this bullet."

Air pulled out an accessory that had been dangling from her neck. It was a bullet, but not a silver one like the Devil's Bullet. Instead, it was an eerie black.

"I am within this black bullet, but I have no clue who resurrected me like this, or even what happened to my corpse. Though, circling back to our earlier topic, perhaps humans do have souls...and mine is sealed in here. Either way, thirty years after my execution, during the second war, I woke for the very first time."

"Seventy years ago..."

The second war...

"Yes, and I quickly realized I had a rather special disposition."

"Disposition?" Rain echoed.

Air paused for a moment. "Do you know the story of the Ten Divine Sentinels from the Bible?"

"Well, yeah."

People considered it a fairy tale, but the story of the Ten Divine Sentinels was common knowledge. Several countries had even derived their names from it.

"Let's see... To defend himself, God chose a representative from each race in the world, allowing them to pick from ten divinities... Also, there's a similar story in an island nation to the far east."

"Yes. So tell me, what was so special about those ten races?"

"I believe it was their divine blessings, which became the inspirations for the names of some countries: Renosaid, the Celestials; Belial, the Daemons; Traxil, the Shieldguards; Rentogral, the Trueflames; Achiral, the Crystalians; Oud, the Grankaisers;

Pharel, the Aviators; Pixie-Oh, the Starspirits; Demifaman, the Demidivines; and Ema, the Lupines. Those make up a total of ten races."

"Correct. And I noticed the brand of the Belial on my body," Air said as she rolled up the sleeve on her left arm.

"That's..."

A pattern that looked like a stagnant black seal was etched onto her arm.

"The symbol of the Belial... As a mage, I've gained a single divinity that exceeds human comprehension."

Divinity was the name for magic that defied human understanding. And the Belial's divinity produced the Devil's Bullet.

"The Belial's divinity... Or in other words, the power of Oblivion. It was...powerful, to say the least. I'd used many forms of Bullet Magic in my life, but the Devil's Bullet was on an entirely different order of magnitude. It was truly a weapon from the age of the gods. And in exchange..." Air paused and lowered her gaze before raising it again and saying, "I became a Ghost."

Her eyes had suddenly changed.

"_____"

Rain couldn't help but feel a chill run down his spine as he watched Air's beautiful, transparent silver eyes turn pitch-black. Black, a color that was impossible for a human. And in the center, her irises looked like rubies.

They were the distorted eyes of monsters, of beasts like the demons and vampires who appeared only in legends and the Bible.

"The color of my eyes is one aspect of this curse. Whenever I use my powers, my eyes become wasp-hued like this. So in order to hide my identity, I have to take great care every single time I use the slightest bit of magic."

Air laughed lightly, but Rain could tell the situation annoyed her. Her black-and-red wasp-hued eyes were simply that abnormal. They were the eyes of someone who deviated from the norm, of someone inhuman. And they all but confirmed she'd lost any last shred of her humanity.

"Well, anyway, seventy years ago, I gave that bullet to the first man I met. I was a genius, so thanks to my life experience, I knew how to best use it," Air proclaimed with her black-and-red inhuman eyes exposed.

Her life experience... She must've meant the life she'd led before she cursed the world.

"I decided to grant this power to many people."

That meant Rain wasn't the first person who'd used the Devil's Bullet. People had had their existence erased many times in the past.

"But unfortunately, I never once found a worthwhile partner. They were all either fools who feared erasing people or who got drunk off the power and destroyed their own lives. Absolute power corrupts absolutely, as they say. If you don't use your head, all that power is a waste... I'd thought my life as a Ghost would never change—but then you appeared, Rain."

Air paused for a moment at that point.

"You're trying to end this war, right? And not in a peaceful, friendly manner. You wish to crush the West so thoroughly that they never dare rear their ugly heads again. That's your goal. Honestly, I like that about you...and I know *exactly* how you feel. You're no mere cadet. Behind that vacant expression is a dark and brutal nature. You'd erase countless others from existence without batting an eye. And I'd wager it stems from the hatred burning in your chest. I'm right, aren't I?"

Intense hatred. Flames of vengeance that coiled upward from the darkest purgatory. Both of those emotions slumbered within Rain Lantz.

"Tch…" Rain clicked his tongue as he restrained himself. He knew if he didn't, his rage would bubble to the surface.

"Well, regardless, you'll have to make a pact with me if you intend to keep using the Devil's Bullet," Air stated as she pulled her handgun away.

"…What does that involve, exactly?"

"I told you already. I desire everything that you are… Or, to put things in simpler terms, I want the right to decide everything you do. If I tell you to go somewhere, you'll travel there, even if you end up in the depths of hell. If I tell you to shoot someone, you'll gun them down, even if they're your family or a loved one. If I tell you to bark, you'll woof like a puppy. And if I tell you to die, you'll drop dead on the spot. All you have to do is act according to my orders," Air said as she playfully twirled the gun in her hands.

"That's…"

How is this not a deal with the devil? Sounds pretty damn devilish to me…

"…Ha-ha-ha. Well, that's fine. I'll give you time to think things through. For now, I'll give you one simple order. If you wish to make a pact with me, complete it."

A deal with the devil… In exchange for your soul, I shall grant you power. Those notions were the stuff of legends, but she spoke of them in an extremely casual manner.

After a few silent moments, Air pulled a piece of paper out of her pocket.

It was a clipping from a public newspaper. The latest publication, in fact.

Peace talks failed.
War to resume after complete breakdown of negotiations.

She'd pulled out an article, and the picture at its center showed important figures from both the East and the West. And standing among them, looking out of place, was a young officer in his twenties.

"See that gentle-looking man there, first from the right? That's a soldier from the West named Alec."

Alec...

"His full name is Alec Thanda. His face may be adorable, but he's one of the most accomplished soldiers in the West. The man is a natural-born warrior who's snatched eight victories from the jaws of defeat. And according to this article, they're going to move him to the central battlefronts because negotiations are going nowhere."

Alec Thanda, an important soldier from the West... Rain had found his next target.

"This is just a provisional order, but I'll speak in an official capacity to help keep us on the same page... Rain, erase Captain Thanda."

The silver bullet—anyone it struck disappeared and left no trace. All their achievements, all the contributions and changes they'd made to the world, were removed from history. Shooting the mother of a hero would undo that hero's birth. Shooting the inventor of a weapon would shift the world into one where that weapon had never even existed.

Reprogramming. That was what Air called these shifts in history. And since he'd gained that power, Rain had used it to end the lives of those who'd left death and destruction in their wake. He'd gunned down generals who'd led great massacres, changing the very fabric of the world.

To this one weak young man, that bullet was both a catastrophe and salvation.

I can change things. I can change everything…

He'd gained a power that allowed him to reshape the world as he saw fit, to put an end to the war.

"……"

As Rain walked through Alestra Academy's courtyard, the shell of the silver bullet weighed heavily in his hand. The almost transparent shell of ammunition had the name of the person whose life it had claimed etched on its surface.

This trace of someone's existence could never come to light. The true power of the silver bullet could not be revealed. Not even to Athly, the partner he'd entrusted his life to on the battlefield.

No one can ever know my secret...

Athly... She was a rather peculiar female student and an Exelia manipulator who'd joined Alestra Academy's training regiment at roughly the same time as Rain. She was fundamentally a whimsical person, but when it was time for battle, she strode through war zones with transcendent operating techniques.

And even putting aside their relationship on the battlefield, she'd been an irreplaceable friend to him since they'd first met. And that was exactly why he had to maintain their relationship as he kept using the bullet.

Rain felt his heart pounding in his chest as he held the Devil's Bullet. He knew if anyone learned of his newfound power, he was as good as dead. And although he seemed prepared for that pressure, when he held the bullet, his hand shivered. Chills ran through him; he was terrified. But still, he couldn't afford to let go of it.

It doesn't matter what I have to sacrifice...

And just as that thought ran through his mind, he encountered someone unexpected.

"Ah..."

He'd been brooding over the bullet in his hand, walking down the west corridor, when he stumbled across Athly among a crowd of people gathered just outside the corridor.

"Athly."

"Oh, hey, Rain."

"What're you doing here? This isn't anywhere near our classrooms."

The third-year students had classes in the east corridor, so she had no reason to be on the west side of the building. However, it seemed Athly wasn't alone. There were around thirty students gathered, some of whom were their classmates.

"Oh, I'm just one of the spectators. Looks like there's someone special in the classroom over there."

"In the classroom?"

Rain stood on his tiptoes to peer past the crowd, and fortunately, he got a peek at the person in the classroom. It was a lone silver girl.

It was Air, to be precise.

"Bwah?!"

"Whoa, what's your problem?!"

The sight stunned Rain. He looked back into the classroom, again and again, praying he'd seen wrong, but there was no mistaking that distinctive look. It was the Ghost girl…Air.

"Ah, aaaaaah?!"

"C'mon, tell me what's wrong! What's in there?!"

Air was dressed in Alestra Academy's uniform, but that didn't make the situation any less confusing. The gaggle of squealing students had surrounded her, which filled Rain with dread. Unfortunately, recess ended right as the thought of doing something crossed his mind, so Rain had to return to his own classroom, where he spent the following lesson fidgeting restlessly.

What. The hell. Is she thinking?!

Why was Air there? No matter how hard he thought, no rational reason came to mind.

★   ★   ★

Two hours passed.

"I'm off!"

"Hold your horses!"

"Ouch!"

Rain stuck out his leg, tripping Athly as she jogged out of the classroom.

"What gives, you jerk?! I smashed my nose on the ground because of you!"

"Where are you going?"

"What do you mean, where?"

Athly hopped back to her feet, seemingly not all that mad about Rain tripping her.

"To see the transfer student, of course!"

"...Good thing I stopped you, then."

"Aw, c'mon, everyone's talking about her! Why not join in on the fun?"

"What fun? Look, just sit tight for now, okay?"

"Huh? What? Why?"

"Don't ask why..."

He didn't want Athly involved with Air. Rain wanted to shield his partner from her at any cost.

Shit, I never expected this. I've gotta think of something...

But what could he do? Rain was awfully confused.

It was their noon recess. The second break since Air had transferred to the second-year classroom. Rain tried to go see her, but she was constantly surrounded by a flock of female students, who made up a mere 10 percent of Alestra Academy's student body.

Due to the screeching girls, Rain couldn't really get a grasp on her motives. There was no getting closer to her, so he never got a chance to question her, either.

Why's she here?

Rain desperately wanted to know the answer to that question. Still, regardless of her reasons, she was not welcome in his eyes.

Why are you letting yourself draw so much attention?

Air had already become a celebrity around the school. Rain had heard everyone in his class, as well as all the people in the hall, spread rumors about the mysterious new transfer student. That morning, Alestra Academy was abuzz with discussion of her.

"Who *is* that girl?"

That was the question every student was dying to find an answer to. And in Rain's mind, that was bad news. She wasn't a normal girl, after all. She was a Ghost who'd been resurrected by magic, a being who existed only in the fires of war. He failed to see what she had to gain by standing out among a bunch of cadets.

She's pretty whimsical, I guess… Is she just doing this for fun? Still, this is a little much.

Air's logic didn't really matter all that much, since the main problem was that she was doing the opposite of lying low. Her hair was silver, and her facial features were adorable, so it wasn't at all odd that the students wanted to get to know her. The whole situation frustrated Rain.

"She's kind of strange, isn't she?" said Athly, who had spent every free moment gathering information on the mysterious transfer student.

"Strange?"

"Yeah. People offered to show her around the school, but she refused to leave the classroom. She even stayed there during lunch, like she was waiting for someone."

Waiting...?

People had already assumed she was waiting for someone.

...This is bad. What the hell is she thinking? Even my best guess doesn't seem like enough.

The more he thought about it, the more curious he grew.

"Only one way to find out..."

Rain decided to go see Air, a whining Athly trailing him all the while. Their destination was the second-year classroom. And once they got there, they noticed that lunch break had thickened the crowd around the girl's desk.

Rain leaned in to listen to what the curt, standoffish girl was telling everyone, but...

"Whoa, what is this? It's delish!"

"......"

Huh?

"Isn't it, Airy?! There's a farm right next door that always gives the students free fresh fruit."

"Wooow, you get to eat apples this yummy every day?!"

"C'mere, Airy. You want some grapes?"

"Yay, grapes!"

"You *really* like sweet food, huh?"

"He-he-he. Only 'cause I don't get to eat sweet stuff too often. Thanksies!"

......

....

"...Who the hell is that?"

"Uh, the mysterious transfer student, duh!"

"No, that's not what I mean," Rain rebuked Athly. "I'm asking who that silver-haired girl getting all the attention is!"

"And I just gave you the answer...," Athly mumbled as she cocked an eyebrow in confusion.

"It can't be. I mean, she's always..."

"Always?"

"No, I mean..." Rain's sentence trailed off as he glanced at the girl who was happily nibbling on an apple.

"Has...um, the silver-haired transfer student always been like this?"

He had to know. Who exactly was she?

"What do you mean by 'always'? She literally just started today! Anyway, from what I've heard, she's very friendly. She always listens, gives considerate responses, and she's all smiles. Everyone's fallen head over heels for her already."

Things made progressively less sense to Rain with every description Athly piled on. He hadn't noticed this morning, but perhaps Air had hit her head or something. Either that or she was pulling off the performance of the century, since she was nothing like her usual self.

She'd hardly smiled whenever they'd met, but she was being so sweet to the people around her that they were turning to mush. And because she was so cute, it was equally effective on both girls and boys.

Seriously, who was she? Even if she was acting, she was doing far too good a job.

At that moment, one girl, who'd been acting all buddy-buddy with Air, said "You know, Air, we have two maneuvering grounds here at Alestra Academy..." as she reached for her shoulder. It was an act devoid of any malice, of course, but she was about to touch her.

"...Shit!"

The moment Rain realized what was happening, his Qualia accelerated rapidly. He remembered Air slamming him to the ground the last time he'd tried to touch her... Remembering how much she hated it, he was terrified.

Is she going to shoot her?

Killing someone over a light touch seemed excessive, but he wouldn't put it past her. Rain reflexively stepped into the class-room to intervene—an act that was both impulsive and unwise.

"Ah."

Her gaze fell on him, and their eyes locked through the crowd of people.

Oh crap... Wait, no. Maybe this is fine.

He met her gaze, stopping Air from reaching for her handgun. However, before he could determine whether he'd made the right decision—

"What kept yoooooou?" Air exclaimed as she lithely jumped like an acrobat over the crowd surrounding her. "I thought my ear would fall off from all their prattling. You should have come sooner."

The temperature in the room dropped as Air whispered directly into Rain's ear. Everyone's eyes gathered on them, but Air didn't seem to notice. Instead, she was confused by his silence and said, "Huh...? What's the matter?"

"What, Rain, you know her?" Athly asked as she approached them.

"Know her? No... Uh, well, maybe a little?"

"Then what are you two whispering about...?"

Air realized the trouble she was in at that exact moment. Turning her head, she saw the multiple lines of sight that were focused squarely on her.

"Oh…"

The amount of attention she'd drawn after acting all meek and adorable had finally clicked.

"…Pfft!" Air laughed. Then she flashed the room a somewhat mean-spirited smile and asked, "What's wrong with all of you?

"I came all the way here just so I could meet you, Rain."

High-pitched squeals from the girls filled the room. But on the other hand, Rain felt a shiver run down his spine.

"Ugh…"

Waves of pure, palpable, murderous hatred rolled off every single boy in the vicinity as they trained their gun muzzles on him.

Later, during lunch break…

"What the *hell* were you thinking?!"

"My word, you're loud. I can hear you just fine," Air responded sulkily. Rain had dragged her behind a mailbox in the courtyard, leaving Air quite displeased. "I'll have you know I was enjoying myself back there. Your face was as red and crumpled as a crushed apple when all the boys chased you around with guns."

"They're *still* chasing us around!" Rain wanted to scream right now.

Girls were an extreme minority at Alestra Academy, so most of the boys hated those who were close to them. The news that the cute new transfer student already had a man on her mind made the boys absolutely livid.

The truth didn't matter. After all, how often did a pretty girl like Air transfer into the gruff military training facility? They wanted to dream of a future with her, but they'd been denied even that faint possibility.

That was why Rain had earned the ire of some thirty male students, who were in hot pursuit of him. And despite all that, he'd somehow managed to grab on to Air and find a proper hiding spot. Of course, she found this hilarious.

They may have been students, but being chased by thirty mages had left him exhausted.

"So why the innocent-schoolgirl act?" Rain asked as he tried to catch his breath.

"Why wouldn't I make myself fun to be around?"

"......"

Is that what you think you're doing?

"Ugh, whatever. For what it's worth, it's just creepy. But as long as no one gets hurt, you do you, I guess... Oh, I do have one question. Why'd you come here? I want a rational answer."

"Didn't you hear me earlier? I came here for you."

"You just said that to mess with me."

"No, that's the honest truth. Sure, I maaaay have deliberately created a misunderstanding because I wanted to make things difficult for you, but it wasn't a lie. That's my only reason for being here."

I came all the way here just so I could meet you, Rain.

"You have the Devil's Bullet, so letting you walk around without a leash puts me at risk. Plus, it's more convenient to stick close to you in case you're ready to form a pact."

"...How'd you falsify your records to get into this school?"

Alestra Academy was an officers' academy run by the country. It was connected directly to the army, so falsifying records should have been borderline impossible.

"The world isn't nearly as well put together as you might believe."

"......"

"There are many methods I could've used. In fact, I even used a different one the first time I came to see you."

Air crossed her arms in a bored fashion, which annoyed Rain. He'd had enough of her insufficient explanations, and he was about to reprimand her, but someone cut him off.

"Whoa, you actually dragged her away with you," Athly said from above them. "I guess you do know the transfer student, Rain."

She peeked in on them from over the mailbox, then hopped down and stood between Air and Rain. After a few seconds, she faced Air to question her.

"So who are you, really?"

"Hey, Athly, this isn't the time or—"

"Zip it, Rain."

Athly silenced him with a raised hand as she continued to stare at the girl in front of her. And Air, no longer in need of her innocent act, gave her a cruel grin in return.

"Oh, I see. Athly, huh...? You're that child from the battlefield... Yes, it's all coming together now. That must be why Rain was so insistent that I behave in your presence while he was dragging me away."

Air was one of the few who knew of the world shifting, so she remembered Athly from the last battle. Unfortunately, Athly wasn't in the same boat, so the discrepancy had created an imbalance in their relationship. It was a unique interaction created by the Devil's Bullet's powers…and due to that, Athly had no way of knowing Air's true personality. Though that didn't stop her from noticing something was off.

"Aren't you acting a lot different around me?"

"Am I?"

"Wow… So what, you were just fooling everyone back there?"

"Shame on them for being fooled," Air said with a scoff.

"Well, that's fine. This is an officers' academy, so they're all tough cookies… Anyway, who are you?"

"Shouldn't you introduce yourself first?"

"I'm Athly Magmet, a third-year student and Rain's partner. You follow?"

"Well, that's good to know, but why should I have to introduce myself to you?"

"Oh, I'm just wondering how Rain knows a little munchkin like you."

"Munch—"

The atmosphere changed; Air was radiating hostility now.

"You're…not his little sister, are you? I mean, even if you are a mage, they wouldn't just accept some random preteen, right?"

"Y-you little…!"

Air shivered angrily as Athly kept dropping borderline insults. And at that moment, Rain realized Athly wasn't speaking out of malice or spite. She honestly just seemed curious.

"If you're trying to pick a fight, don't bother. I…"

"Wait, what? Who's picking a fight with who?"

"We're! The only people! Here!"

Losing her patience, Air got in position to pounce. However—

★   ★   ★

"All students are to stow their weapons at once."

"I repeat. This is an order from third-year prefect Orca Dandalos. All students second year and below are to stow their weapons immediately."

"That's..."

"Orca."

It was a message from the class prefect, Orca, who was trying to calm Rain's pursuers.

"I understand wanting to pump Rain full of lead, but we cadets cannot codone the unchecked use of force. It's only natural to be angry at a skirt chaser, but we can't just mob him and string him up."

"Orca..."

The hidden daggers in those words hurt Rain, but he was still grateful for the save. A prefect had spoken up, so chasing him was a clear violation of—

"That's why I'll set a proper stage, with rules in place, to help you work it out."

"Huh...?"

"All third-years are free until two PM, right? Participation is completely unrestricted. Anyone who wants to make some quick cash or beat the stuffing out of that skirt-chasing prick should gather in the third-year classroom right away."

With those words, the broadcast cut—

"Oh, and Rain, you have to participate. I'll kill you if you don't show up."

And with that final remark, the broadcast cut off. For real, this time.

"Yeah, of course."

Ten minutes later, forty-odd cadets gathered in the designated classroom.

"I've got something real good on me. Check out this Centra gun."

A small stir passed through the classroom.

"A Centra? No way!"

"I probably don't have to tell you, but this baby's an old automatic pistol. You can use it during live combat, but it's also an antique with a high price tag. It's a first-generation, premium item, branded with the year 1822. Any noble who knows his guns will fork over eight hundred thousand for this bad girl."

The classroom stirred again. Eight hundred thousand zels was a fortune. Rain could hear students gulping in anticipation.

Orca smirked in satisfaction at the attention focused on him, then continued, "It's also a memento from Second Lieutenant Risma, who passed away recently. Their dying wish was for this gun to go to a promising young soldier. Sadly, there's only one pistol, so we can't split it…which leaves us with only one choice… Let's start a contest over this babyyyyyy!"

""""Yeaaaaaah!""""

Everyone in the classroom cheered in agreement.

Orca started his briefing.

"The rules are simple! Thirty minutes from now, we'll hold a mock battle in the main building! We will, of course, be using blanks! If you're hit on any part of your body, you're disqualified.

Once time runs out, we'll hold a final match between the four competitors with the highest kill counts!"

"Same rules as always, then!"

"That's right!"

Everyone seemed to be on board.

"What about sneak attacks?"

"Allowed!"

"And teaming up?"

"Allowed!"

"And double-crossing?!"

"*Totally* alloooooooowed!"

The students were discussing a bullet royal, an age-old tradition at Alestra Academy. It was a battle royal in which contestants used low-firepower Bullet Magic for sport.

Traditionally, it was a last resort used to settle disputes, but this year's prefect, Orca, hosted them rather often.

"Also, this goes without saying, but any damage to a person's body or property is permitted as long as it doesn't exceed the set threshold."

"Meaning?"

"You can beat the stuffing out of anyone who pisses you off, no problem!"

""""Yeaaaaaaaaaaaah!""""

"Hold up—there's *definitely* a huge problem here!" Rain protested, but his words were drowned out.

Rain had been forced into the bullet royal. He wasn't actually interested in it at all, but over half the participants were out for his blood, so he couldn't sit back and wait to see how things would shake out. The whole thing was a mock battle in form, but given how close it was to a personal dispute, which was otherwise forbidden, his life was at risk.

Most participants seemed hell-bent on gaming the system to take potshots at him and settle their grudge. The group that had been admiring Air had already formed an alliance, even. Though they weren't the worst of the lot...

"Eight hundred thousand... *Eight hundred thousand*..."

"I can pay it back, pay it all back, with two hundred thousand to spare... He-he... He-he-he..."

Ugh...

In Rain's eyes, the people who wanted to sell an officer's memento for some quick cash were scum.

"C'mon, didn't you hear him? That gun's a memento! Where do you get off selling something like that?" Rain snapped at his classmates, who were getting into position.

""Shuddup!"" Kenth and Euroia, who formed an Exelia pair, both screamed at him.

"Kindness doesn't fill your wallet."

"What can gratitude buy you?"

"I can't believe how serious you two look when you say that."

They were truly misers at heart.

"I'm warning you now, if I get a clear shot, I'll beat you black-and-blue!"

"Yeah, what he said. I've been mad at you for stealing Athly since we enlisted, but you were both so into each other that I could let it slide. But now I find out you have another girl on the side? I swear, you deserve to die once or twice..."

"Not that you can really die more than once."

Rain looked around. Out of the forty cadets present, ten had their sights set on him.

Dammit, this is bad. I can't believe they're all after me. What a bunch of idiots…

"All right, guys, you'll hear the signal in one minute. The battle starts then."

Everyone scattered as soon as Orca finished saying that, and a minute later, a gong echoed through the building.

Thus, a battle royal with an expensive memento and a personal grudge on the line began.

"…Guess I'll hide."

As soon as the game began, Rain expended his stamina to escape the people hunting him. As a result, he reached the library without anyone noticing him.

During bullet royals, the library was always completely deserted, since it wasn't directly connected to the main hall. Only kills a person scored directly counted toward their point total, so hiding was pointless. Proactive play was the best route to the finals.

In that way, it was different from a regular battle royal, in which hiding until the end was a sound strategy.

Rain fully intended to hide from the group that was targeting him, but he also planned to switch gears and go for some kills once the heat was off him.

Once he felt confident he was safe, about ten minutes after he took cover, Rain began scouring the library.

"I have some time to kill, so I may as well see if I can find anything."

He was searching for a book to help him put the previous day's events in context…

I was executed by the military…

He recalled what Air had said.

He couldn't tell how true those words were, and he didn't actually care, either, but after the way she'd inserted herself into his life, he needed to find out more about her.

And so he looked into records of the first war. Alestra Academy housed tomes filled with national military records, meaning he easily found what he was looking for, but…

"…Shit."

As he'd thought, Air's name was nowhere to be found. Records showed that the East had ended the war with a spectacular come-from-behind victory, but the details were sparse. The records stated only that the East had avoided defeat.

The information was scrubbed…

The lack of information annoyed Rain. Air was rushing him to make a decision, so he desperately needed to know more.

Rain, erase Captain Thanda, she'd said.

Alec Thanda, a man regarded as one of the most valiant warriors of the West. Even with the Devil's Bullet on his side, Rain wasn't entirely confident in his ability to defeat him. It still wasn't clear when the man would launch his attack, but Rain knew he probably had less than a month… So before then, he had an important decision to make. Would he let go of the Devil's Bullet…or would he make a pact and bind himself to the silver girl?

I have to come up with a plan…

Right as that thought crossed his mind…

"Found one!"

"Ah!"

The library door slammed open, revealing Athly. She had a rifle in her hands and was clearly looking for targets.

Oh, this is actually pretty convenient.

He'd wanted to speak to Athly privately, and they were all alone in the library, so this was the perfect opportunity.

"Hey, Athly, can we talk for a—?"

Bang!

"Bwah!"

A bullet flew toward him.

Holy shit!

She'd shot at him without even looking his way!

"H-hold up—it's me, Rain!"

"...Huh, Rain?"

Athly finally recognized him, it seemed. However, she kept her rifle trained on him, her finger hovering over the trigger.

"If you're going to beg for your life, go do it in hell!"

"Wow, we've got a real badass over here."

That was a pretty cool line, I gotta admit.

"Wait, forget all that. I need to talk to you about something. Hear me out."

"What, you trying to weasel your way out of a loss?"

"I'm serious, Athly. This is important."

"If you're just going to beg for your life... Wait, what?" Athly seemed startled. "Something...important?"

She visibly wavered, then began lowering her gun.

Now's my chance!

"Right. This is an *extremely* important issue, and I've been meaning to talk to you about it for a while now."

"I-important..." Athly's shoulders jolted, and her attitude changed. "You've...wanted to tell me...something important... for a while now...?" she whispered to herself as she looked down at the ground.

"Um..."

"What?"

"Is it...about you and me...?"

After saying those words, she paused for a moment before continuing with "And our relationship...going forward?"

"Bingo. I'm surprised you figured it out."

That's some impressive intuition. I tip my hat to you, Athly.

"So can we talk now?"

"Is it something you can't say...unless we're alone?"

"Well, it'd probably be better for you if we did this with no one else around."

"Ah...!" Athly finally lowered her gun all the way as she let out that sharp gasp. "C-can you give me a minute?!"

Then she turned around, pulled out a small compact mirror, and started using it to fix her hair. Once that was done, she wiped her sweat off with a handkerchief and made sure her hairpin was on just right.

As he watched her, Rain realized that Athly definitely was, without a doubt, a girl. A strong-willed, cute girl who looked out of place with a gun in her hands.

Why's she doing this? Is this really the time to fix her hair...? Well, whatever. Doesn't look like anyone else is around, at least.

"S-sorry. I kept you waiting, huh?!"

Athly finally sat down after getting her reddish locks in order.

"So, um. What is it."

"...Why're you talking like a robot?"

"No reason! So what's up? Also, I'm just putting this out there, but I prefer it when guys are direct!"

She'd made herself clear, so Rain would work with her on this. "Well, in that case, I won't beat around the bush. Let's call things quits. There's someone else I want in my pair."

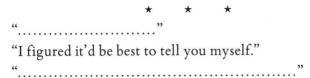

"...................."

"I figured it'd be best to tell you myself."

".."

By *pair*, he meant a team made up of a gunner and a manipulator who piloted an Exelia together. Athly had been his partner ever since they'd enrolled at Alestra Academy three years ago, but things had changed.

The Ghost, Air, was a part of the picture now. He hadn't made his decision yet, but he didn't want to drag Athly into his mess if he ended up accepting Air's proposal. It wouldn't have mattered if Athly was an average manipulator, but her skills were transcendent. She was far too good a soldier to be wasted on his crusade, so finding a new partner was to her benefit. However—

"U-um..."

It took Athly a fair bit of time to form a coherent response.

"Wh-why do you...want to do that?"

"Why? Well, I mean..."

What was the best way to answer that question without mentioning Air? Sure, she'd shown up in his classroom before, but the Devil's Bullet's Reprogramming had made sure no one remembered that. Plus, he hadn't agreed to work with her yet, so he had no choice but to come up with an ambiguous response.

"There's someone else I want by my side."

That was when it happened.

Bang!

"Huh?!"

A bullet zoomed past his ear...and the very next moment, Rain heard the sound of glass shattering.

"Eek...!"

Athly had just shot at him.

"I can't believe you!" Athly cried as smoke rose from the barrel of her gun. "You ended things before we even hooked up!"

"Quit yelling! I'm the one in shock here, you lunatic!"

Why the hell'd you shoot me?! Have you lost your mind?! I know they're just blanks, but they can still break bones at close range!

"Oh, it's fine, Rain."

"What's fine?"

"That was a real bullet."

…Come to think of it, she was aiming her personal handgun at him instead of the bullet-royal rifle.

Wait, how is that a good thing in her mind?

"Say, Rain, I heard an interesting story recently," Athly said, holding her gun steady.

"Wh-what?"

"Apparently, there's a country where cheaters get cut into four pieces."

"I'll put aside the question of who exactly cheated here, but… yeah, I've heard that. They say both the cheater and their paramour get cut in half. That's an interesting story, all right."

"It is. And that's why I want you to bring them to me. This person you're so interested in."

"Huh, what for?"

"Don't you get it…?" Athly asked before she paused and took a deep breath. "I want to punch two new holes into you!"

"Whoa…!"

"C'mon, Rain, why?! Where'd this come from?" Athly was regaining a bit of her sanity and started her interrogation in earnest. "We've been a team for three whole years now! We've worked so hard together to this day! And now you're going to throw all that away and team up with someone else? That makes no sense!"

"Saying 'to this day' kinda makes me think you've already given in…"

"Ugh…"

Alestra Academy had no official Exelia pairs, since there was no telling what role one might need to fill on the battlefield. However, Rain and Athly were somewhat of a special case, so people around them knew they were best left to their own devices. And the two of them also thought changing partners was too much work, so they'd never bothered.

Rain saw this as an opportunity for both of them to grow, which was why he'd suggested it.

"Ugh, are you sure about this?"

"It's a good chance for you to polish your skills, so yeah."

"That's… I don't know if I agree with that."

"Oh?"

"Who'll be your next partner?"

"Uh…"

"Are you going to team up with that girl?"

Athly was being vague, but it was rather obvious whom she was talking about.

"That…pretty, silver-haired girl."

That was a natural assumption, given he'd asked her to break up their team the same day Air had transferred in.

"No, it's got nothing to do with her. I've actually been meaning to have this conversation for a while now."

"But you'll be pairing up with someone new, at least temporarily, right?"

"I mean…"

You're not wrong...

He hadn't thought of whom to ask yet. He had options in his class, but only high-ranking cadets were sent to battlefields. And out of that select group, the only one he knew he could work with was...

"...Orca. I'll probably ask him."

"Fine, I understand."

"What do you understand, exactly?"

"That if he disappears, all will be right with the world."

Athly's parting words stabbed into Rain's heart. Yes, they were in the middle of a battle royal, but she wouldn't *actually* kill him... Would she?

Making a person disappear...

Those words rang all too clear within him.

Time had run out.

"For the time being, I'll announce the people who've made it to the finals."

All the bullet-royal contestants had gathered in Alestra Academy's central plaza.

"That said, only four people survived, so they automatically move on. First place is yours truly, Orca Dandalos, reigning at the top with eight kills. Cry your eyes out, you losers!"

"Die!"

"You useless muscle-bound jerk!"

"Baldy!"

"Hey! What smart-ass called me bald?!"

If this had been a wrestling match, Orca would've been the heel. Not only was he class prefect, but he also won one out of every five bullet royals, so quite a few people hated him. Unfortunately for him, he seemed more exhausted than usual, so his chances this time seemed slim. And the reason for that was…

"Second place is Athly Magmet, with six kills! Except…"

"Mmmgh…! Nnnnnngh…!"

"She kept trying to shoot me even after time ran out, so the other girls had to restrain her."

Orca poked his thumb out toward the girls who were pinning Athly. Her eyes were bloodshot as grunts and moans escaped her gagged mouth.

"Rain."

"Yeah?"

"What's got her so worked up? She chased me around for almost the whole match," Orca whispered into Rain's ear.

"Well, the weather's nice today. Maybe that's why," Rain replied nonchalantly.

"…Fine, whatever. Third place is Rain Lantz, who weaseled his way in with two kills."

"Die!"

"Die!"

"Die!"

"C'mon, can't you at least be more original?!"

People seemed to hate him just as much as they did Orca, but the gap in effort was depressing. He understood why they were angry, too, since no one had managed to punish him for his perceived misdeeds.

"And fourth place, with the same number of kills, is the new transfer student, Air!"

"Yay!"

""Yeaaaaaah!""

Orca's words were soon drowned out by the male students' cheering. Air had donned her facade once more, acting out the part of a perky schoolgirl and driving the crowd wild.

Rain walked up next to her. "...Hey, how long are you gonna keep up this charade?" he whispered into her ear.

"Where's the harm in it? They seem to like it."

"Why are you even participating? You don't care about that gun."

"I'm bored."

There were no restrictions on the event, so anyone was welcome to join. Still, everyone, Rain included, had been shocked when Air had asked to participate. But the true surprise came later, when in the final minutes of the match, Air rapidly closed the gap by taking down two random, unsuspecting contestants.

Seriously, what's your angle here?

"Rain, should we really let her participate?"

"Well, it looks like she's up for it."

"You sure she'll be okay, though? She may have qualified for the finals, but she'll end up getting hurt if she's not careful."

"It'll be fine. She might act all cute, but I know she's wild enough to beat down a gorilla with her bare hands."

Whack!

"Ouch!"

"Hmph!" Air harrumphed as she kicked Rain in the shin.

"What gives?!"

"You bumped into me."

"...Well, okay. The final four contestants are me, Athly, Rain, and Air."

The finals were the main event of any bullet royal—a four-way battle, one on one on one on one. Individual Bullet Magic was allowed, putting the level of danger above that of the qualifier; there was no time limit; and a person was eliminated as soon as an attack connected with them.

"By the way, since we're doing this out on an open plain, you can't use your Bullet Magic, Rain."

"That's no fair! You're cheating."

Not that I wasn't expecting this, but it still sucks!

Rain's classmates all knew he favored the use of Pharel's rebounding shots, which were rendered useless when they had nothing to bounce off.

"You're not even denying that you're cheating... I mean, come on, you guys can use Pharel, too!"

"We can, but none of us can control that suicidal shot."

"...Fine, whatever, open plain it is."

"Cool, let's get started, then."

At those words, the girls released Athly so she could go prepare. Luckily, she'd calmed down after being pinned for so long.

"......"

That said, the way she sullenly rose to her feet was terrifying. Rain thought about saying something, but the palpable aura of murder wafting off her was so strong that he didn't dare approach her.

"Right. Everyone ready?"

All the contestants checked their gear. Athly had an adaptable automatic WR handgun. Orca used some unknown shotgun. Rain, as always, used his BB77 revolver. Air pulled out one of the guns she carried on her back, a medium-sized rifle of unknown origin.

Bullet Magic was divided into many branches, all of which included several variations. That was why Rain stepped in as Orca prepared to fire the opening shot.

"Hey, Orca. Could you let me fire the opening shot?"

"Huh? Well, sure, but why?"

"I'm using a revolver, so I can point and fire, but you've got a shotgun, so you'll have to change your grip."

"Uh, I guess that makes sense?"

Orca relinquished the role of firing the first shot to Rain.

"Okay, let's get started."

Rain's Bullet Magic zoomed through the air with a shrill bang, marking the start of the bullet royal finals.

The very next moment, the whole area was flooded with a light so intense it even shone through one's fingers. Rain had fired an Ozette, also known as the "White Flash" spell. It was Bullet Magic that interfered with the environment, blinding any who happened to see it. Sure, it lasted less than three seconds, but Rain was capable of reloading faster than any of the other three, and he had more than enough mana to rapidly fire more bullets.

Using the time he'd bought, he ran up behind Athly to take her out. Every gunner's blind spot was behind their dominant hand, and that rule held just as true for mages. However, as he prepared to take his second shot, Rain's Qualia ordered him to freeze.

"Ugh..."

A strong current of electricity that was powerful enough to smash through rock poured out right in front of him. If he'd taken another step, it would have hit him directly. That was a form of Bullet Magic: Libertas, or the "Rapid Thunder" spell.

"Nice intuition."

Athly knew how to make expert use of that elementary Bullet Magic. She'd covered only the fundamentals, since she specialized in Exelia manipulation, but she'd still turned something so basic into a deadly weapon. Unfortunately, that wasn't enough.

"Shit...!"

"You're too slow," Rain said as he stepped toward her. Instead of magic, Rain employed a simple grapple. And after pinning her pistol to her, he stepped back and kicked Athly's abdomen.

"Ugh...!"

She tried to elbow him in the face in response, but the blow barely skimmed his eyelid. He was bleeding, but he grabbed her body and lifted her up all the same.

"No, aaah!"

After a moment, he slammed her into the ground, chest first, at full strength. She stayed down. But unfortunately for Rain, Ozette dispersed as soon as he finished, revealing Orca standing there with his shotgun at the ready. The two of them stood there, staring at each other, with their Qualia active...

Do I move...?

Orca had deployed his weapon's sight. Heat sizzled as it gathered in the muzzle.

Shit, suppression magic?!

The multiple bullets Orca unleashed into the air above them puffed up, their mass doubling several times over.

"Horgo Bardas!"

Orca's Bullet Magic rushed forward with the power of the "Meteorstorm" spell. Heavy, jagged rocks appeared above Rain, forming a savage shower of stones that reduced the ground to dust within seconds of impact. The number one student at Alestra Academy was powerful indeed. But that intensity of his was also his weakness...

"Sorry, Orca."

"What?!"

"You spent too much time looking at your bullets, idiot!" Rain exclaimed as he appeared behind him. However, Orca loaded a second shot and switched to defense faster than Rain could shoot.

Orca A. Dandalos was the prefect at Alestra Academy, the most prestigious officers' academy in the East. He boasted powerful Qualia, backed by innate talent and a massive well of mana that set him apart from the pack. And on top of all that, he was familiar with Rain's Bullet Magic. Victory was within his grasp so long as he used his future sight to predict the trajectory of any bullets Rain fired. Pharel's rebounding made that job harder, but considering the lack of any terrain to bounce things off, he didn't have to worry about that.

But the moment that thought crossed his mind...

"Urk!"

...a bullet hit the *back* of Orca's head.

"H-how...?!" Orca asked as he collapsed, turning to look at the bullet that had flown in from behind him.

"Oh, about that... It's the bullet I fired to start off the finals."

Rain had asked to fire the opening shot instead of Orca for a reason. And he'd fired that shot *horizontally*, at low speed, so it would eventually bounce off the main school building and pierce Orca's head.

"...Asshole."

"Shut it, loser!"

Rain pumped a final shot into his good friend's abdomen to end his run. And having finished off both of his closest friends within ten seconds, he turned around to face a silver figure.

"Aaaah..." Air let out a carefree yawn. "Well, I see you stick to the ironclad rules, if nothing else."

"What ironclad rules?"

"Taking out the weakest enemies first, of course."

As she said that, Air moved her finger over the trigger of her rifle. And then, with a low voice only the two of them could hear, she continued, "A pity, though. I wanted to take out that Athly girl myself."

"Because she called you a kid?"

"……"

Air's expression shifted from uninterested to displeased. She'd always seemed detached, aloof, and distant, but this was different. It seemed as if talk of her childish build had soured her mood.

"Do you think…?"

Rain just barely made out what she was saying.

"Do you think I want a body like this?"

What…?

A shadow fell over the girl's face. The withering disdain, as well as the artificial smiles, all slipped away…revealing a bitter expression. It was the same look she had whenever anyone tried to touch her.

That face…

Did it mean she loathed him so much…? No, there was no mistaking it. That was surely an expression of…anguish.

"Hmm…"

Air had said she was born over a century ago. And her existence had been sealed within a small bullet upon her execution, enabling her to appear as a Ghost whenever war broke loose. Rain wasn't sure how that had happened, but he did know that her body was by no means natural.

Which begged the question, who had made her body? How did she have a physical form? The more Rain thought about it, the more doubts surfaced in his mind, leaving a gap in his defenses.

"Ah..."

As a mage, he had to keep his Qualia up to predict attacks from any possible angle.

She's making her move.

Air moved to attack Rain.

"Ugh..."

As they were surrounded by spectators, his actions were a bit restricted. Still, he predicted a large barrage of bullets rushing at him as he charged her, so he twisted his body to avoid it. And as soon as he did, a bullet flew by above his head. That was Air's Bullet Magic. Flames blazed up from the point of impact, but that wasn't enough to stop Rain, since he'd escaped her range... However, the next moment, a shadow blocked his field of vision by rushing at him.

"Uh-oh!"

Another prediction assailed him.

I'm in danger!

He'd instinctively guarded his abdomen, but right as he had, a bullet had struck his body from above.

"Urk, aaah!"

A training round burst against his abdomen, sending Rain tumbling to the ground. Any attempt to rise to his feet was rendered impossible by the waves of pain running through his body.

"Sh-shit..."

As he crawled along the ground, he heard a distinct clicking sound coming from above him.

"Four seconds," Air said, her tone entirely casual. And it remained flat and devoid of any emotion as she continued to look down on him.

"You're a little too weak, aren't you?"

A sneer crept into her words at that point. But upon raising his face, Rain noticed something was off.

Why...are you so...?

Why was her expression so sad?

Her lips were pursed, as if it took all she had to swallow down her emotions. And yet, her eyes were so moist that any onlooker could tell she was putting up a brave front.

She seemed to be on the verge of tears.

What the hell, Air? What are you...? Why do you have that look in your eyes? What are you hiding from me? You won't tell me anything, and whenever I touch you...you get hurt and won't ask for help. How selfish...

"See you later."

Her casual good-bye was followed by a loud gunshot. Rain lost consciousness as he took a blank to the head.

5. PACT

Leminus had grown around Alestra Academy. The capital of O'lt-menia had no room to accommodate an officers' academy, so one had been built nearby, and that had attracted all sorts of people.

Its population was roughly a third of the capital's, but the town still flourished, developing thanks to both external and internal trade of ironwork and other local goods, earning it the moniker the "Iron City."

Due to its proximity to Alestra Academy, many students used the town to restock their supplies. And on this day, Rain, along with another dozen or so students, had changed into casual clothes to pay it a visit.

"We're gonna meet back here at noon, got it?" Orca ordered.

And with that, the students scattered across the city. Since Alestra Academy's students knew state secrets, they needed to apply for the privilege of visiting Leminus. As such, their rather infrequent outings were almost vacations.

The cadets often lacked free time, and they were running over to assorted hobby shops and restaurants with Orca in the lead. Rain, however, slipped through the stream of classmates and headed toward an antique bookstore.

Hmm...

Books were stacked haphazardly across the shelves in the store, but there was also a rather large collection of old newspapers. And Rain had made it his mission to scour through all the ones from a century ago.

"I didn't expect much, but still…"

While looking through the large collection of old newspapers, which were encased in thin glass to prevent any degradation, he'd found what he was looking for.

"…Bull's-eye."

Major battle between cadets and Lenox military.

Major step forward. Military headquarters to mull over the benefit of manufacturing more arms.

"Guess it wasn't a lie…"

Air had told him the truth. One hundred years ago, at the tail end of the first war, a group of cadets had saved the East. But at some point, reports on their achievements had suddenly ceased, which served as ample proof of the military suppressing the information.

That didn't prove Air had led the unit, but it did instill a sense of confidence in Rain. He was convinced that the girl who'd called herself a Ghost truly was, in fact, someone from one hundred years ago.

After coming to that conclusion, Rain ordered copies of a few articles from that time period, then returned to town.

"Oh, Rain."

Rain had noticed Athly as he gazed at a fruit store's display.

She'd ready to leave the town square, but she stopped and turned to face him when she got close.

"Done with your shopping?"

"Yeah, I picked up a few magazines and some cold compresses. By the way, Rain…"

"What?"

"Today's actually my birthday."

"Oh…"

"You don't have to sound so annoyed!"

"No, that's not it, really!"

Rain wanted to celebrate with her, but this trip was his chance to learn more about Air, as well as Ghosts in general. Alestra Academy had limited records, which he'd already pored over, so stores in Leminus were his only other option.

Well, I guess I have some spare time.

He'd noticed that Athly had been plagued with anxieties on the battlefield as of late, so he hesitated to brush her off. Ever since he'd gained the Devil's Bullet, he'd forced Athly through battle after exhausting battle, barking orders at her nonstop.

The Devil's Bullet had the ability to completely erase a person's existence, but the fact needed to remain a secret. Which was why he'd kept it from Athly. All those factors had come together to create an extreme sense of guilt.

"Well, in that case, you have anything in mind?"

"I sure do!"

"Actually, I already picked something out. It's over here!"

"…You picked something out?"

Athly had dragged Rain over to a jewelry store, then asked

him to buy her one of the items sitting in the showcase. It was a hairpin with a rather high price tag on it.

"Ugh…"

It's really *expensive.*

It cost 100,000 zels. Even Rain had to admit the blue pin was cute, and Athly was showering him with thank-yous, but…

"Do you really want it that badly?"

The price was outrageous. The shop's owner was an amicable middle-aged man who realized they were cadets and tried to present them with cheaper pieces, but Athly stuck to her guns. And eventually, Rain gave in and bought her what she wanted.

However, for some odd reason, Athly refused to have the hairpin wrapped, and she started doing her hair in the middle of the store.

"You're gonna put it on here?"

"Well, how often do I get presents? I don't want to wait until I get home."

Pulling her hair together, she put it into a ponytail. And after she added the pin, she asked, "How do I look?"

"Wow…"

She looked like the kind of attractive girl Rain often saw around town.

"You're pretty damn cute when you act like a normal girl, you know that?"

"It's no act. I *am* a normal girl!"

"Do you *seriously* believe that?"

"Of course I do. I'll leave it like this when I go home, then."

"Home…" Rain suddenly remembered something. "Your family lives here in Leminus, right?"

"Yeah…"

Home… Athly's expression had clouded over as she'd said that.

"I enrolled at Alestra Academy against my parents' wishes…so I figure I should go home every once in a while to reassure them. Show them I'm doing just fine."

"…Yeah, it's probably best not to worry them."

"Mm-hmm… Still, I don't intend to go back permanently, no matter what. A lot of my relatives were killed by the West. If I don't keep them safe, Mom and Dad could be next."

That was Athly Magmet's reason for joining the army. And it was an extremely simple, common one at that. People close to her had been consumed by the fires of war…and her parents were the only survivors.

"Thanks, Rain. I'll catch you later," Athly said as she finished fixing her outfit, then promptly left the store.

Rain waited for her to get out of earshot, then turned to the jewelry shop's owner and started talking to him.

"Listen…"

"Hmm?"

"Can you lower the price of that hairpin at all?"

"You pathetic boy…"

A hundred thousand zels is too damn expensive!

"Please. I just wanted to show off for her!"

"They say honesty is a virtue, but…ugh, fine. I'll knock off ten thousand for you."

"Wow, really?"

He'd only asked because he had nothing to lose, so that response was unexpected.

"You're Alestra Academy students, right? Consider this my way of saying thanks. You're putting your lives on the line at such a young age, so I owe you one. Besides, she's your girlfriend, isn't she?"

"…It's more like a crush, really."

"Mmm... Well, don't give up the fight. Next time you come to me, you come for a ring."

They continued that vague conversation for a few minutes longer, since the owner had a tendency to ramble. But he ended up with a *fifteen* thousand zel discount, so it was all worth it.

Rain left the store a good twenty minutes after Athly. And then *it* happened.

"Huh?"

Rain couldn't believe his eyes.

An Exelia stood before him.

He recognized the armored vehicle made of graimar nuclear alloy, a formidable weapon of war. The humming of the combat machine was especially terrifying here in such a peaceful town. And it wasn't one of O'ltmenia's units, either. It was a newer AT3 model from the West.

"No way..."

It was an enemy unit. The moment Rain realized that, he noticed the upheaval in the town around him. People were panicking, rushing around in random directions to escape the chaos.

The Exelia moved before Rain's eyes. Its gunner aimed at the fleeing masses and fired a *certain bullet* into the air.

Wait, that's...

The black bullet was shaped like a small, lean metallic tube. The shot flew so sluggishly that watching it could distort one's entire sense of time. But eventually, the black tube burst, unleashing a massive wave of heat.

"Shit!"

Leminus, the Iron City, was engulfed in flames.

★   ★   ★

It's hot...

Something felt incredibly heavy.

U-ugh...

His hazy consciousness gradually cleared, but his sense of smell recovered far before his sight.

"Urk, ack...!"

Miasma infiltrated Rain's nostrils—the scent of something burning. Rain's dim thoughts spurred his body into action, but no matter how many times he tried to move, he failed to get up.

When he tried moving his back, he realized something was on top of him... A burned corpse.

Fuck...

The size and shape suggested that it was the remains of the jewelry store's owner. Someone he'd spoken to mere moments ago was dead. The man hadn't been a mage, so he'd been unable to cast defensive magic to shield himself. He'd been reduced to an unrecognizable state by the heat.

Ugh, shit...

The gruesome sight of the melted corpse made Rain sick to his stomach. But he knew if he didn't move, he'd be next. So he resisted the overwhelming nausea and crawled out from under it, taking stock of the situation.

What...the hell...?!

A ridiculous number of corpses were among the rubble. Hundreds and hundreds of charred, burned bodies were spread out as far as the eye could see. And the fire raged incessantly, fueled by the blood of the innocent. But worst of all for Rain, the scent of burning flesh and the smell of gunpowder made it impossible to breathe. The noxious air was far too thick, so he had no chance to catch his breath.

With a thud, an enemy Exelia landed in front of him. Its fuselage was covered in soot and blood, showing off the slaughter it had committed.

If I don't run now, they'll kill me…, Rain thought as his heart thumped in his chest.

He knew that for a fact, but his body refused to budge. His uncontrollable trembling left him rooted to the spot. He realized then just how afraid he was.

He'd fought through several battlefields, but even so, he'd very rarely felt the imminent presence of death. There was no escape for him. Exelias were the peak of military technology, so there was nothing his mortal body could do.

The enemy unit's gunner trained his sights on Rain, signaling the end of his life.

"What…?"

However, at the very last moment, another unit rammed the AT3, knocking it away.

"Get in, Rain!" shouted an amplified voice.

Finally shaking off the shackles of despair, Rain broke into a sprint and hopped into the Exelia that had rescued him.

"We're withdrawing immediately!"

Athly was at the helm of the vehicle. She turned away from the enemy AT3 without so much as giving it a second glance and took off.

"I'm sorry. I put you at risk."

"Don't worry about it. Let's just focus on gathering the rest of the cadets. Oh, and hang on tight!"

Athly easily outmaneuvered the enemy, giving Rain a newfound appreciation for her skills, and eventually escaped them entirely.

"Wait, what about your parents?"

Athly had mentioned her parents lived in Leminus, so they may have been in danger. With losses this heavy, Rain doubted they'd escaped, but he wanted to make sure.

"They're fine. My parents took cover in the underground shelter... But forget about them for now—let's just go."

"Go where?"

"To everyone else."

Athly accelerated. During their journey, they caught sight of another AT3 unit. And while turning to avoid it, they saw it indiscriminately gunning down fleeing civilians.

Rage boiled within Rain as he reached for his gun.

"Don't," Athly warned him calmly without turning around, convincing him to stay his hand. "It'd expose our location."

"Dammit..."

Rain suppressed his emotions as soon as he heard her explanation. She was right. Provoking them was a surefire road to death.

After driving through the ruined city for a while, Athly rammed their unit into a ravaged hangar that was half-buried by rubble. Except, as it turned out, the rubble was merely camouflage, and the unit broke through the thin veil to enter a wide chamber. Waiting there were their classmates, the cadets of Alestra. Maybe twenty of them in total.

"So this is where you hid them."

"There's no telling when they'll find us, though."

Find us...

"So they've really..." Rain trailed off, unable to finish that question.

"The West has launched an attack on the city, yes," Athly replied.

"Right. They've brought Exelias into a civilian area. And more than just one, too. They're running all over the city, gunning down any person they find. It's unheard of, strategically speaking." Orca added his own explanation. It seemed he was in charge of the place.

What few weapons they had were gathered in front of him. It was appropriate enough, since Orca was the prefect, and he'd been trained to take command during emergencies.

"The enemy's objective is to seize this town... No, scratch that. Their objective is to sack the town and slaughter everyone in it."

A slaughter... The recent sequence of defeats had put the West in a rather precarious position, so it had changed its tactics to retake the initiative. And unfortunately for them, Rain and his classmates had gotten caught up in the mess.

This was the Iron City, Leminus, a harmless commerce area located far from the front lines. And that meant the attack was a premeditated attempt to claim innocent lives.

All the cadets understood that fact.

"So what do we do next?" Rain inquired.

"I dunno. What can we do?" Orca replied.

"Fleeing isn't an option. The ground around Leminus is flat, so there's nothing to stop their Exelias from running us down."

The cadets had only a single Exelia, which was an older model the town had gotten for self-defense purposes from Alestra Academy. Its specs were subpar, and they'd escaped the AT3 earlier only because of Athly's skills.

"We have two choices in front of us," Orca stated. "The first one is to hide. If we make it to nightfall or wait until the enemy retreats, we might survive. Though I doubt reinforcements will make it here anytime soon, so I don't see them retreating. Plus, there's no guarantee we'll survive until tonight…"

Orca paused to let that choice sink in before he presented a different one.

"Our second option is to bail immediately. It's risky, but if we make use of the chaos, we could just slip by."

In other words, hide or make a break for it. That was it. The cadets had only one Exelia, so combat was out of the question. If the enemy discovered their hideout, they were as good as dead. But regardless of which path they took, they needed a firm grasp on enemy movement. And so, at Orca's behest, everyone observed the surroundings through their monoculars.

Five minutes later, Bangas Rover, a rather timid individual who didn't leave much of an impression, reported something.

"Th-that's…"

"What is it?"

"Oh, uh, I've been scoping out the main street…and I think the enemy's command unit is stationed there."

Everyone gathered around him and looked in the direction he'd specified. Just like he'd said, there was a large group 650 feet to the west. Ten operating Exelias were stationed there, with six storage vehicles in tow. That was *definitely* the enemy's command unit.

One vehicle among them had its windshield down, and Rain spotted a familiar face behind it.

"That's…"

"You know who that is, Rain?"

"…Yeah."

He'd only seen him in pictures, but he was sure of the man's identity. After all, he was the subject of Air's order.

"Alec…"

Captain Thanda, the only western soldier who'd amassed victories as of late. He'd been present when peace talks had broken down several days ago, and he'd advocated decisive action.

He must've orchestrated the attack. He was the one most responsible for this atrocity. And upon recognizing the man's presence, Orca and the rest of the cadets reacted poorly.

"He's so close by…"

"They'll kill us… If they find us, we're toast."

"No, we're cadets, so they may take us hostage."

"You seriously think they're gonna take prisoners? No, they'll put us down like dogs."

Sheer terror filled their minds. Understandable, since even a single AT3 was more than enough to deal with all of them.

But one among them was different.

Captain Thanda… What should I do?

Rain was frightened, but he remained undeterred. He had an ace up his sleeve, a card only he could draw. He firmly grasped the Devil's Bullet, mulling over what to do with its power.

Do I use it…?

Orca had listed two choices. One was to wait; the other was to run. But in this situation, Rain, and Rain alone, had a third option. He could fight.

If I erase Alec with this bullet…

The warrior of the West, Alec Thanda, had launched an attack on a peaceful town, resulting in the slaughter of thousands. Based on the scope of the operation, the West had probably sent at least fifty Exelia units and over three hundred soldiers.

On the other hand, Rain's side lacked resources. They had only fifteen cadets and an out-of-date Exelia…

Don't panic. Think…

Rain gathered all the combat experience he had to help form a plan.

Can I use it?

He'd used the Devil's Bullet hundreds of times already. And by erasing people with it, he'd turned the tide of the war in his country's favor. The bullet made assassination a cinch, since he could use it to remove any obstacles entirely.

Reprogramming was a rather unique phenomenon… Instead of just killing a person outright, it erased their existence, along with all their accomplishments. And that made it perfect for the situation at hand.

Erasing Alec would undo the massacre in the town, saving thousands, so it was the logical choice in Rain's mind. The only real question was how to best achieve that goal.

Can I shoot him from here?

No, he could not. Alec was barely peeking out of his unit, and he had no reason to leave it. Plus, even if he did exit his Exelia, Rain was too far away to land a clean hit.

And the most important factor of all was the price he had to pay to use it.

"You'll have to make a pact with me if you intend to keep using the Devil's Bullet."

Rain had to strike a deal with that silver-haired girl to keep this power.

"If I tell you to shoot someone, you'll gun them down, even if they're your family or a loved one. If I tell you to bark, you'll woof like a puppy. And if I tell you to die, you'll drop dead on the spot. All you have to do is act according to my orders."

The next time Rain used the Devil's Bullet, he would relinquish all that he was to her. But regardless of Air's involvement, Rain had no chance of reaching Alec.

"Orca, what weapons do we have if we try to make a break for it?" Rain asked, hoping to get out of this deadlock.

"Just some guns. There's some interesting stuff in here, but we can't use it..."

"Like what?"

"See those sacks next to the Exelia?"

"What about them?"

"They're full of solid gunpowder. The kind you process to make bullets."

The cadets were holed up in a depot owned by the military, so the presence of munitions wasn't much of a surprise. Gunpowder could serve as an explosive, a weapon of sorts, but...

"It's no use."

...Orca had clearly already considered that option.

"There's a decent amount, but it's all old stuff that was sent here for disposal. We can't load it into cartridges... Besides, gunpowder isn't even all that useful on its own."

Gunpowder was usable only when processed in airtight conditions, so they were better off sticking to Bullet Magic. Any attempt to use the old Exelia and a bunch of trashed gunpowder was sure to end in failure.

Unfortunately, as Rain was mulling over such thoughts, the situation took a sharp turn for the worse. The sun shifted in the sky, changing the angle of its rays to stream directly into their shelter.

"Hey, get away from the rubble! You'll reflect the light!" Orca shouted.

However, his warning had come too late. The light filtered through the rubble, reflecting off the lens of one of the monoculars.

Aiming with one's back to the sun was fundamental sniper knowledge, but they'd seemingly forgotten it in the chaos.

"Get down!"

The next moment, a blast hit the wall of rubble. An enemy gunner had noticed them and fired Bullet Magic without pausing for thought. The attack claimed the lives of three unsuspecting cadets who'd failed to duck.

Three of their classmates had been reduced to bits of flesh, their faces blown off and their upper halves torn apart. And Rain could tell through the dust that the enemy was approaching to search for any stragglers. Based on their movements, he could tell they were unsure whether there were any survivors, but that would only last as long as the dust clouding their vision.

"Wh-what do we do?!"

"W-we've gotta run!"

"Where?! We can't outrun an Exelia!"

"Well, what do you suggest we do, sit on our asses and let them kill us?!"

The cadets were breaking. They may have been military personnel, but they were still young students. Seeing their friends' gruesome end had unnerved them.

We're gonna die...

But that was the one thing he wasn't willing to accept. And as he grew more desperate, Rain's *eye* throbbed as if it was about to burst.

"Ah...!"

He covered it with his hand to help calm the pain and...

"Air!"

...suddenly called out the Ghost girl's name.

★   ★   ★

The rest of the cadets calmed down, startled by his scream.

"You're watching all this, aren't you?!" he shouted furiously. Before the echoes had even faded, he continued speaking to the girl he couldn't see. "Be honest—you're laughing your ass off, aren't you?! I bet you're grinning like the devil himself!"

Rain clutched his hoarse throat and took a deep breath to calm his cracking voice.

"I hate to admit it, but I can't get out of this on my own. I'll make your damn pact! I'll give you everything I have! All that I am! So grant me your power!"

He took a deep breath.

"Save me, Air!"

"You didn't have to yell all that…"

The voice came from behind him through the cold air, like a wisp of fog.

"I can hear you just fine…" The silver girl had appeared before him at last. "Well? Happy to see me?"

"You really were watching us…"

"Yes. And I'd say you're lucky I was."

"So what do you say?" Showing no regard for the other students staring at her, the girl turned to address Rain directly. "I take it you're ready to make a pact?"

"Yeah. I'll give you everything. Just do something about this mess."

"I swear, you are so needy…"

Air sounded rather disappointed, but Rain could tell that was all an act.

"Well, whatever. I'll show you what a dependable master I am.

That should convince you I'm worth serving. Just remember, you can no longer take back your words. From now on, you belong entirely to me, Rain Lantz."

She paused, then moved her hand to her skirt.

"Do you want another peek, to mark the occasion?" Air asked as she fluttered her skirt about in a flirtatious manner.

"I'll pass."

"What a shame. Looks like you're not quite ready on that front."

Her attitude was as flippant as ever. It honestly made it hard to believe they were in a life-or-death situation. This Ghost, this mysterious girl called Air, was an oddity. After smoothing her skirt back down, she pulled out a pistol and fired a single bullet straight into Rain's chest.

"I call it a pact, but this is really all there is to it."

Rain couldn't tell whether she'd actually fired a bullet, since he felt no pain. But a moment later, a crimson pattern etched itself onto his left arm. It was the mark of the pact, the very same symbol of the Belial as the one on Air's skin...

"That pattern, the Jisknot, is the link that binds us."

Rain had gained a clear, tangible connection to Air.

"So long as I live, you cannot disobey my orders. It's something of an incomplete master-slave relationship."

"...Incomplete?"

She can order me to kill myself and I have to obey...and it's still incomplete?

"...How is this any different from a deal with the devil?"

"Well, if I die, all the magic I possess will transfer to you, so you always have the option of slitting my throat while I sleep. You do have a way out of it, so I can't claim to have all the power in this deal, can I?"

"That's…"

It seemed Rain had a card to play. If Air died, all her magic would transfer to him. Including, of course, the Devil's Bullet.

"What will you do? Do you wish to try your luck already?"

"…No," Rain replied resolutely. "Being a slave suits me just fine…for now. Please just do something about this situation already, Air."

"Very well, then. Let's get moving."

Having concluded their discussion, Air walked off toward the cadets' only real weapon, a certain old Exelia.

"Get out. I'll take the wheel."

"Huh? What?" Athly muttered, clearly confused. A normal reaction, since she didn't know a thing about Air's background.

"Just listen to her, Athly."

Athly stepped down from the platform, heeding Rain's request. With her out of the way, Air boarded the Exelia, but the other students weren't so keen on handing over their last line of defense. After all, their lives were on the line, and they were all on edge. They wanted to speak up and stop her. However—

"Hear me, students of Alestra Academy!"

Her voice was cold, nothing at all like her amicable facade at school, and it stopped them in their tracks. She had adopted the stalwart tone of a warrior who demanded absolute power and authority.

"I am Air Arland Noah, the one who will lead you to victory in this battle. I have no time to explain everything point by point, so I will simply tell you our objective. We shall gun down every last soldier of the West."

Air's declaration was loud enough to reach everyone, but that didn't make it any more believable.

"I-is that even possible?!"

"No way! Do you realize how outmatched we are?!"

The cadets shook off their terror and started raising complaints to her orders.

It was impossible. It was reckless. They understood the situation they were in, so this was a natural reaction. But instead of responding to them, Air grabbed the gunpowder sacks with the Exelia's auxiliary arm, loaded them onto the platform, and ordered Rain to get in behind her.

Rain hopped in as instructed, but he had no idea what her plan was.

What the hell is she thinking?

Still, that was his only real option.

I have to bet it all on her.

Air had declared she would lead them to victory. Everyone else had deemed the situation hopeless, yet she seemed entirely sure of herself. So he decided to risk everything right then and there, since the alternative was sitting idly by and awaiting death.

The Exelia roared to life and crept forward.

"We'll break through the rubble and rush them."

Air paused for a second, then rammed the Exelia straight through the wall of rubble. The maneuver was rather bold, but it was also the most effective way to surprise their enemy.

Their single, isolated Exelia surged toward the enemy, kicking up clouds of dust and showing no hints of stopping. Air prepared to face the enemy troops, but they'd already sensed her and her unit coming with their Qualia. Their future sight was guiding them down the optimal path.

Air and the enemy had chosen to face each other with Bullet

Magic, a mage's weapon of choice. In this battle, each blow would be powerful enough to be a killing stroke.

Air drove her Exelia forward until she and one of the enemies were in range of each other. But the next moment, right before the two were about to collide, she pumped the brakes.

"So slow."

"Whoa, aaah!"

Rain yelped in surprise at the sudden jolt—and then he realized their unit was entirely airborne.

The Exelia had jumped.

The enemy was stunned, and rightly so. Exelias were made out of graimar nuclear alloy, an extremely heavy material, and they *definitely* weren't equipped with any mechanisms that allowed them to jump several feet though the air. However—

I see, this unit is…

It was an older model, meaning it was lightweight. Its motor was feeble, and its armor was thin, which made it less effective in combat, but that also enabled some wild stunts. By using the rubble as footholds, Air had pulled off a less-than-graceful jump that almost looked like a mistake.

Frankly, it was a spectacular feat.

But unfortunately, Rain's Qualia was now screaming at him about imminent danger.

Shit…!

Another unit had noticed their presence and fired off Bullet Magic in their direction. But Air remained undeterred.

"This is child's play."

Air deftly dodged the oncoming barrage, sliding by effortlessly and never slowing her forward charge. Her skills were transcendent.

What enemy units remained shifted to defense, firing volleys of suppressive fire, but she evaded them all and reached the enemy's main force in the blink of an eye.

"Jump out, Rain."

"Huh?"

Air's instructions had confused him.

Jump out?

"Yes. You need to complete our little diversion. Jump from the unit and take care of the rest."

That did little to explain, so Rain gave her a questioning look.

"Shoot *this unit.*"

A mere second later, Air grabbed Rain by the scruff of his neck and threw him out of their Exelia. Rain plummeted toward the ground with a new case of whiplash after being dropped from a vehicle that was traveling at over thirty miles per hour.

And as he fell...

"Wh-what...?!"

"Go on, shoot!"

...the truth dawned on him.

Shoot? No way...!

He'd figured out what Air was planning.

She'd told him to shoot *their* Exelia.

I get what she's trying to do, but this is pretty damn reckless!

Rain followed her orders and aimed at their Exelia's platform...where the *sacks full of gunpowder* were.

"Here goes nothing!" Rain exclaimed as he fired his bullet.

The next moment, a powerful explosion rocked his eardrums. The large stock of gunpowder had unleashed enough kinetic force to destroy five enemy units.

Black smoke trailed up quietly for a while after that. The

cadets watched everything from behind the veil of that ebony smoke screen, standing in dumbfounded silence. And as they did, Air arrived to shock them to their senses.

"See? We did it. While you were all busy bemoaning how futile the situation was, we took action and claimed victory."

The silver Ghost had returned to their hideout in the rubble after soundly defeating the enemy. And after a momentary pause, she tossed Exelia activation keys at the cadets.

"Now choose, children."

These keys would start the mobile weapons she'd just stolen from the enemy. When she'd taken their transport vehicle, she'd found several spare Exelias in perfect condition inside.

"Are you pigs for the slaughter...or wild boars who will fight?"

This silver girl, this wandering Ghost born of a tragic death, urged them forward.

"Whether you rise to the occasion or cower in terror is of no concern to me. However, if you choose not to oppose them when you have weapons in hand, when you have the means to strike back, you'll remain pigs forever. And all livestock meet the same end."

Slaughter.

"This situation may seem bleak, but you lot are in luck."

There was no real logic behind that statement, but that didn't matter.

"If you put your lives in my hands...you will emerge victorious."

Air had gained everyone's trust with a single gesture.

Rain shuddered with awe at Air's tactics.

"Gyk, prepare for bombardment. Tactical Unit Three is approaching you."

"Requesting support. Luvain and Elan's unit to point N3."

"Catch them in a pincer attack, boys. Oh, Orca and Centonal, make adjustments for a wider firing angle. Once the enemy turns around, rush them. They won't run away."

Air's voice came over the common communication line as she dexterously directed the six Exelias they'd obtained.

"Hey, Rain. Soon enough, we'll pass by two enemy units who are currently three hundred thirty feet south from here. They'll be in your firing range. Blast them away," she brusquely called.

She was instructing him to shoot down enemies who hadn't even arrived yet... Normally, Rain would've ignored her, but he knew not to doubt Air.

"And...here they are."

Rain focused his energy on the two enemies that appeared. When given enough time to prepare, a mage had the power of a fixed cannon. They could unleash powerful Bullet Magic any-where within their effective range.

A beat of silence.

Rain's Qualia activated. And following Air's orders, he unleashed an attack to ward off the encroaching enemy. A massive blast of fire erupted near them. The enemy evaded it, dodging the close-range attack, but...

How predictable...

...the second shot that followed, Rain's Pharel bullet, penetrated and severely damaged one unit's engine, while another burst into flames from the third bullet he'd fired at almost the exact same time.

She'd made suppressing such a powerful strategic unit look so easy... *Too* easy.

This Ghost...is a monster!

"Good work. Remain on standby until further instructions. Oh, and look after River and Garudo while you can."

Even as she instructed them to remain on standby, Rain mar-veled at how different she seemed. It was hard not to be amazed. After pillaging the enemy's equipment, she'd handed the cadets five Exelia units. They were state-of-the-art machines, but Exel-ias required teams of two to properly operate, so the enemy still had them hopelessly outnumbered. And yet, she'd used what little resources she'd had to turn the tide.

She's gained control of this battlefield already...

Air's leadership had shown results almost immediately. Alec Thanda, commander of the western forces, had stopped the attack on the city to focus on the cadets. But that hadn't changed any-thing, since Air had defeated wave after wave of enemies. She'd turned the tables; the hunters had become the hunted.

This is insane…

The power of a Ghost was overwhelming. It was beyond all mortal comprehension. Air hadn't even employed any special tactic; she'd simply overwhelmed the enemy with her keen mind.

Air was terrifying. She didn't have the Devil's Bullet or any special brand of magic at her disposal, but that didn't matter. Sheer intellect, along with her Qualia, allowed her to control the battle.

However, as Rain stood there in awe, admiring Air's skills…

"Rain, do you copy?"

Athly's voice crackled through the radio. She'd been sent out as a decoy to distract as many enemy units as possible.

"What's up? Is something wrong?"

"No, if anything, it's all going so smoothly that it's kind of scary. I mean, we've got no losses on our side! Anyway, there's something I'm not sure we should report to that girl... Air. That's why I'm checking with you first."

"What is it?"

"Well, they're all empty..."

"What does that mean?" Rain didn't understand.

"All the enemy units we've been fighting so far? They're empty. No one's on board."

What…? "What the hell does that mean?"

"Exactly what it sounds like. Our Exelias took out three enemy units that were part of a larger group, but no one was actually in any of them."

"…Unmanned units?"

That made no sense. Unlike Rain, who'd been firing from a

distance, Athly's group had gotten up close and personal. They would've noticed if there was no one behind the enemy's windshields. But when they checked the units after taking them out, they found no traces of people in the wreckage.

"......"

Had the West completed work on Exelia drones? The concept of an unmanned system had existed since the invention of Exelias, but that was all it had ever been—a concept. Rain pondered Athly's report, trying to work out a plausible explanation.

"What do we do? Should we tell her about the unmanned units?"

"Yeah..."

Even if Rain and Athly doubted the validity of the information, their superior officers had to be briefed. That was an ironclad rule within the military. So Rain told Athly he'd report it himself, then cut the comms.

......

An Exelia was a complex quadruped machine that could be operated only by a mage. Sure, the West's research and development had advanced considerably further than the East's, but it was hard to imagine that it had created autonomous units.

What was the alternative, then?

Unmanned units, a sudden raid from the West, and...a Ghost.

There's something there...

It felt like things were finally clicking into place, like he'd gotten all the information he needed to form a proper answer. A shudder ran through Rain, as if he'd just been doused with ice-cold water.

Am I...overlooking something?

Rain was sure he had all the pieces of the puzzle, but he didn't know how they fit together yet.

What's going on? What the hell am I missing here?

He started to feel extremely impatient. Rain's instincts screamed at him, telling him to figure it out already. However—

"Hey, Rain."

A voice from the radio pulled him back from his thoughts, but it wasn't Athly this time around.

"I'm heading over to your position now, so take cover."

It was a transmission from Air.

She's coming to me?

Before Rain managed to completely process her words, a cloud of dust formed behind him. A several-hundred-pound lump of metal had landed there with a thud.

And as he turned toward it, his eyes fell on an AT3 unit. Air's unit.

"Good work, Rain."

"...This is the third floor."

Rain had been sniping enemies from up in a dilapidated building, and it went without saying that Exelias didn't have flight functionality, so her sudden entrance on his floor was extremely odd.

"What, you gonna tell me that flight magic is a real thing now?"

It felt like a stupid question in his mind, but his curiosity had gotten the best of him.

"What are you saying? No magic can make Exelias fly."

"But that's the only possible explanation..."

"It certainly isn't. I don't need any magic if I have the proper footing." Air lightly stomped the ground as she said that to punctuate her point.

"...You climbed up the wall."

"I did."

A vertical climb up a wall with an Exelia was an insane feat; her explanation was near unbelievable.

"Are you really so ignorant? It would be impossible for a manipulator of average skill, but this armored vehicle packs a lot of power. Some people out there can scale walls with no equipment, right? It's the same principle."

"……"

Rain had a lot he wanted to say about that, but he recognized that it wasn't the time or place to speak up.

"So what do you need me for?"

"I found Alec. It's time to take him down. Now get in the back seat."

They were going to settle this battle for good. All they had to do to fix things was erase the person behind the massacre, Alec Thanda.

"Can we really take out Alec?"

"Of course we can. I spent the last hour trying to track him. For better or for worse, Alec is no fool. He refuses to show his face, but I managed to calculate his position by working backward."

Rain followed her orders and settled into the gunner's seat.

I should probably tell her about the unmanned units…

He wanted to warn her, but unfortunately—

"We're climbing down the wall."

"Huh…? Whoa!"

The Exelia's front wheels rotated, and it slid down the wall of the building. The shock from the sudden descent made Rain forget his earlier thoughts.

This maniac is…actually sliding down the wall…

He was utterly dumbfounded by her near-impossible maneuvers. Their Exelia moved and revolved like a living creature, avoiding any and all obstacles in its path. And while they were making their way along, Air started to talk to Rain.

"You know, you really are quite skilled."

"Huh? What do you mean?"

"I'm saying you're a good shot. I've thought as much before, but this just confirmed it. You have the mind for it... In fact, one might say you have a good *eye* for this," Air commented. It was clear she was implying something.

"...How much do you know?"

"Who, me? I don't know anything. To me, you're just a fun toy. Nothing more, nothing less."

Rain knew she was playing dumb.

"Hey..."

"That said, you honestly excel far *too* much. While I was busy trying to smoke out Alec, I noticed that the number of enemies had decreased considerably thanks to your efforts. But the range you'd hit them from was unbelievable."

Rain had downed five enemy Exelias on his own, which was most unnatural.

"Your effective range is two hundred twenty-five feet. That's a difficult distance to shoot with a rifle, but you pulled it off with exceptionally potent Bullet Magic. And it's far beyond what any ordinary cadet could do. You're an unprecedented case."

Air peered directly into Rain's eyes, her gaze intense and piercing. It seemed she knew something was unusual about them...

"...If you keep staring at me like that, I'll have to start charging you for the view."

Rain turned away from her in an attempt to hide his right eye.

"Ha-ha-ha-ha, I see... I'm starting to understand how you managed to kill hundreds of officers with the Devil's Bullet. You're fueled by your wrath, your hatred of the battlefield... At your very core, you..."

She wasn't wrong—wrath and hatred did indeed fill his heart. But why?

"Well, I suppose I can ask about that later. It's almost time."

As soon as she finished her sentence, Air turned on the comms and started barking out orders.

"Levis, travel another six hundred and fifty feet north-northeast, then shoot a burst shell at the blue civilian structure.

"Luvain's and Athly's units, proceed to form a diversion. Keep the enemy units at your position."

Three seconds after that instruction, Rain saw his target.

"Is that...?"

"Yes."

Rain had spotted several enemies.

"The unit surrounding Captain Thanda consists of two rigs serving as his escorts. He's in the third one, so we have a total of three enemy Exelias."

The enemies were fast approaching, with only about 325 feet remaining between Rain and the enemy's main forces.

"I'll get us in as close as possible, so be ready to snipe Alec at a moment's notice."

Right, Alec is my main target...

Rain braced himself; right now, he was armed only with regular Bullet Magic because they weren't yet close enough to use the Devil's Bullet. Air accelerated their unit a moment later, closing the gap swiftly. They'd entered each other's firing range at last, beginning Exelia combat.

However, a sudden explosion filled Rain's field of vision.

"What the hell?!"

An enemy unit...had detonated, creating a chain reaction that destroyed all of the units around Alec's. And Rain wasn't at all responsible for any of it. The shots had come from the enemy's own allies.

"Wow... Now that's an interesting escape plan!"

The enemy commander, Alec, had fired on his own subordinates. And by the time the smoke and dust of the explosions had settled, he was nowhere to be found. He'd mercilessly used the lives of his comrades as bait.

No, wait...

Rain noticed something between the flames. The units Alec had just destroyed were all *unmanned*.

All the enemy units we've been fighting so far? They're empty. No one's on board.

Athly's words rang in his ears. But they were no longer mere words, since he'd seen it with his own two eyes. He continued to observe the scene, and as he did, he caught sight of his target.

There he is!

Rain spotted Alec through the flames. He'd escaped into a nearby abandoned building.

"I'll chase him down, Air."

A second later, Rain jumped out of the Exelia and took off after Alec on foot. Air kept shouting something at him as he ran, but he ignored her, prioritizing the enemy.

As soon as Rain set foot in the building, he was surrounded by thick smoke. Alec had clearly set a magical trap to disable his pursuers. But Rain remained in the building, exposed to the brunt of the miasma, and activated his Qualia to predict Alec's whereabouts.

There weren't many places to hide in such a small space, but it still took him a while to catch Alec.

"Found you!"

He stood at the center of the second floor.

"You are Captain Thanda, aren't you?"

"...I am. Seems like you've got the right person."

From up close, Rain noticed that the young man was much thinner than he'd expected.

"Tell me—who are you?"

He left an odd impression, as his hair was dull in color and his gaze was devoid of warmth. The man was rather scrawny, especially for a military man. As he stood there casually, he seemed almost out of breath.

"I'm impressed that you managed to corner me. Your Qualia really is something else," Alec said, completely composed. "I didn't think there'd be a cadet...or any human, really, who could see through my actions."

"You..."

"You are a cadet, right?"

There was no heat, no passion, no sense of bloodthirst in this man.

...*Who the hell is this guy?*

As he faced Alec, Rain could feel a stomach-churning sense that he should not involve himself with this man. It wasn't just rejection... It was terror. He couldn't make sense of his behavior at all.

Does he...really have his back against the wall?

An abnormal sense of enmity prickled against Rain's skin. Standing face-to-face with Alec made Rain especially sure of the situation. He'd hunted Alec down and trapped him, but for whatever reason, he felt like the helpless prey caught in a trap.

It was the same feeling as when he faced Air... No, it was worse this time. Rain's intuition screamed, warning him of the *inhuman* being before his eyes.

"Amazing."

Alec directed his gaze at the ceiling, which only made Rain more nervous.

"To think I'd lose to such a perfect strategy. How did you pull it off?"

"I don't have to answer that question."

"This whole situation is abnormal. I've never faced such a sound defeat."

Alec didn't lift his gun, but that didn't mean he was defenseless. After all, mages had their Qualia on at all times in battle. It allowed them to derive the optimal solution when faced with danger, so it was the ultimate defense. This was a battle between mages, so Rain had to play along until he got the upper hand.

"Who are you?"

He knew he had to continue the conversation with Alec, the man behind the massacre.

"No, that's the wrong question... You're not the leader, are you? I can tell."

"That's..."

"You don't have to answer that."

Alec cut Rain off, telling him not to bother.

"...I see. It all makes sense now. Things went entirely as predicted... Well, in that case..."

"What the hell does that mean?"

"You're the Belial, aren't you?"

A long, drawn-out pause settled over the room.

"Yes, I can tell by the look on your face that I missed the mark entirely. Well, damn... I guess that goes to show how lowly I am... I thought it was impossible, but it actually turned out to be true."

"Alec, what are you…?"

"What, am I wrong?" Alec asked.

"You have one of *these*, don't you?" He rolled up his sleeve, exposing the skin of his left arm. "The mark of the Daemons, the Belial. It should be just like my mark of the Grankaisers, the Oud."

A seal was etched onto Alec's upper arm.

The Oud's brand.

It was strikingly similar to the brand on Rain's flesh, a sigil of providence.

"Why do you have that…?"

It was the mark of a Divine Sentinel, a secret only Rain and Air shared…

"What an odd reaction. Don't tell me the silver girl kept you in the dark about all this?"

"…Silver? You know Air?"

"Know her? What are you saying?"

"We're both Ghosts. I could never forget the face of an enemy I've fought for so long."

The warrior of the West, Alec…
The Oud…
We're both Ghosts…
Fought for so long…

Rain finally understood what had been bugging him about the whole situation.

Right, why did Air specifically order me to erase Alec?

Sure, Alec was a soldier with an exceptional service record, a perennial thorn in the East's side, but that wasn't enough to make him a high-priority target. The West had many other people on par with him.

So why did Air choose him, of all people?

They're both Ghosts... That's what he just said, right?

Rain had figured out the truth, but the revelation had come too late.

Alec lowered his head, and when he lifted his face, his eyes... had turned black and red.

It can't be...

Rain had witnessed the phenomenon before, so he knew it all too well—this horrifying transformation, those diabolical eyes that could freeze the very blood in a person's veins.

Whenever I use my powers, my eyes become wasp-hued, turning black and red.

Alec had undergone the exact same transformation as Air.

"You've left yourself completely unguarded," Alec stated as he moved on Rain. Then he pulled a handgun from a holster on his waist and fired a bullet out of the building. It looked as if he'd missed his mark, but that wasn't the least bit true. He'd planned that shot all along. And a few seconds later, Rain's Qualia activated, letting him know *exactly* why.

"Ah...!"

Rain felt a shock wave erupt above his head, and the ceiling caved in. Several dozen tons of rocks started falling on him.

"Fuck..."

Alec had decided to bury Rain alive. Large piles of rocks spilled into the building, and through the opening, Rain could see what had broken the ceiling.

"...What the hell?"

An Exelia smashed through the ceiling, ramming directly into the floor. And just like earlier, it was *unmanned*. But that wasn't

even the oddest part... The machine's engine had been destroyed during the crash, and yet somehow, it still moved.

"Very impressive. As I thought, you have good intuition."

A chill ran down Rain's spine when he heard those nonchalant words of praise.

"Now let's see how you deal with the next one."

As soon as Alec uttered those ominous words, the floor under Rain's feet started rumbling. A second later, flames and shock waves at his feet knocked him off balance.

"Urk, aaah!"

"Ha-ha-ha, you don't even need the staircase anymore!"

Rain crashed down to the floor below, landing right next to a lone mage with a rifle. It seemed that mage had shot through the ceiling to strike at him.

Goddammit...

Alec had prepared an ambush, Rain realized, and he reflexively prepared to counterattack. But as soon as that soldier entered his field of vision...

"Huh?!"

...Rain lost his will to fight. Which made sense, since the man was missing half his body.

What the hell?!

Rain doubted his eyes. The soldier held a rifle in his right hand, but his left was nowhere to be found. And before Rain managed to come to grips with the situation, the man crumpled to the ground and stopped moving.

Wh-what...is this...?

There was no mistaking the sight. A *corpse* had shot at him. Rain desperately held back the urge to jump up in fright.

He calmed his nerves, then focused on the man's body once

more. Had it been blown off by a sniper shot or torn apart in a blast? Whatever the case, the fact remained that he was dead. There wasn't any blood dripping from his torn appendages, and his heart was missing, so he shouldn't have been able to move.

That soldier had long since passed. And yet, until just a few seconds ago, he'd been moving.

What is this...? What the hell is happening?!

Exelias moving on their own, a corpse firing at him—all these things shouldn't be able to move, and yet they were.

Impossible...

No magic or technology could've caused any of that. But what if...that odd phenomenon was the result of a *special* power?

"The Oud's property is called Enthrallment."

"Ah..."

"It allows me to enforce orders on any targets my bullets pierce."

Startled by the voice, Rain turned around to see Alec ambling toward him in a calm, composed manner with his pistol in hand.

"It's not limited to people, either. Machines, animals, corpses... I can force a target to do anything, as long as it can physically handle the task. It's the stuff of dreams... Though I'll admit, it's inferior to the Belial's divinity."

Alec released the shells from his revolver's chamber to prepare his next rounds. They looked similar to Air's bullets, except they were gray.

Those are...

The gray bullets Alec employed, which packed a special power.

"It allows me to enforce orders on any targets my bullets pierce."

Anything could be manipulated. Unmanned machines, living humans, or even the dead were all fair game in his eyes.

What the hell is this guy?

He had the same unusual Bullet Magic, the same black-and-red eyes. And most importantly...he called himself a Ghost. Rain wanted to know more about the man so similar to Air. However, survival was his main priority. He had to avoid getting caged like an animal.

"I finally understand," Rain said as he cast aside his doubts, recalling the mission he had to accomplish. "I can't win this fight without killing you. I've got tons of questions on my mind, but I'll have to put them aside for now."

"What?"

Alex didn't comprehend Rain's words.

"Your life ends here, Alec Thanda. You've killed too many innocents."

"Hmm... You intend to win, eh? How admirable. So enlighten me—what tricks do you have up your sleeve?"

Alec wasn't the least bit frightened. He knew Rain possessed a minuscule amount of mana, so he was confident in his victory.

Rain hated to admit it, but Alec was clearly a far more skilled mage. If he'd fought him head-on, he'd have been reduced to cinders in mere moments. However, that hadn't happened, and Rain had also noted the arrogance Alec displayed at times.

He isn't...

He wouldn't deliver a killing blow... Over the course of their exchange, there had been several times he could've ended Rain's life. But instead, Alec had simply watched and laughed as Rain scrambled helplessly. Alec had decided to toy with Rain, thinking he had the option of finishing him off whenever he wanted. But that carelessness, that arrogance, would be his downfall.

Rain fixed his eyes on his target, aimed his gun at it, and said, "Fine, I'll use it."

Then, he fired his bullet diagonally to the right.

"Ha-ha-ha-ha! What, have you gone blind now?!"

He'd fired in a seemingly random direction, completely miss-ing Alec. And because he assumed Rain had made a mistake, Alec didn't budge an inch.

Good… Stay right there!

The shot he'd fired to the side was the silver bullet. It hit the back wall at a thirty-four-degree angle, then the adjacent wall at fifty-five degrees, the upper section of the wall at seventy-seven degrees, and the lower section at seventy-five degrees, ricocheting against the roof tiles, rebounding, ricocheting, rebounding, rico-cheting… It went on and on until he saw it.

"What's wrong? What are you going to—? Gaaah!"

"You were too careless, Alec."

He saw Alec get hit. The silver bullet had bounced around countless times to avoid Alec's Qualia before settling into the back of his skull, which sprayed fresh blood.

"If you'd focused on your Qualia the whole time, you could've avoided it."

The Devil's Bullet ended Alec's life. And as it did…

"Ah…"

…the world shifted.

"Urk, aaah!"

The world had undergone Reprogramming due to the power of the Devil's Bullet.

"Did I…shift over?"

A second ago, he'd been in a dilapidated building on the north side of Leminus with Alec. But when everything changed, Rain found himself in…

"Where…am I?"

...a completely unfamiliar place.

Looks like I'm still in Leminus...

After looking around, he realized he was in a wide cellar with no windows. There was a staircase in the corner, and he could see the familiar forms of his classmates. Except...

...What's wrong with them?

Something was off. His classmates were all silent, hugging their knees. None of them seemed injured, but they looked dead inside.

What happened to them?

"......"

Rain moved to check what had happened. And after ejecting the magazine from his rifle, he confirmed that the shell had the name Alec Thanda etched onto it.

What's happening...?

The shell was proof that the world had shifted, erasing all of Alec's deeds. But if that truly was the case, why were his school-mates hugging their knees in a cellar? The enemy commander had been expunged from the annals of history, and that should've averted the massacre. Leminus should've been at peace, but...

"Hey...tell me what's going on right now!"

Rain approached Centonal, who was squatting with his head down. Like Orca, he favored fire Bullet Magic, and he was a strong-willed individual with firm character. But even he was shivering like a scared kitten that had lost its parents.

"Wh-what do you mean?"

"Just tell me, Centonal. What happened here?"

"F-fuck off! Now's not the time for your stupid questions!"

Centonal seemed extremely flustered. He *definitely* knew something, but Rain didn't think he was in any state to answer questions. So he checked with the others, but none of them were in their right mind, either.

This can't be... What the hell happened here?!

Something terrible had obviously occurred, but he'd run out of leads. Giving up on them, Rain rushed up the stairs...and saw something that shocked him to the core.

"Wh-what *is* this?!"

Scarlet-red fire raged... Leminus had been consumed by crimson flames.

"Why...?! I erased Alec!"

A sea of red flames had spread as far as the eye could see. Leminus had become little more than a smoldering inferno. Alec's existence had been erased, but the fire burned down the town with even more intensity than the destruction that had preceded it.

However, the biggest difference of all was the *color* of the flames burning the town.

Crimson...

It wasn't a pillar of normal fire. Instead, it was a thick, true shade of red, a deep scarlet that left an intense impression on all who beheld it. And amid that conflagration, Exelias rushed through the town. Mages fired Bullet Magic that destroyed civilian homes, murdering any citizens who flocked out of them in a panic.

This once peaceful, sleepy town had been dyed red by the raging flames, as well as the flesh and blood of its inhabitants.

Rain couldn't understand the situation at all. What was happening? Why was the fire even worse than before the world had shifted?

As those sorts of thoughts ran through his mind...

"Hello."

...someone called out to him.

"Huh...?"

★   ★   ★

"Are you...a Ghost, too?"

When Rain turned toward the source of the voice, his gaze fell on a girl. She stood with her back to the flames, like the personification of the destruction itself.

"No, you're not. I see... You're Air's..."

The girl was so red, it was almost ridiculous. Her transparent eyes shined with an inhuman ruby glint as she directed a void-like gaze at Rain.

But the next moment, those eyes...

"Well, it doesn't matter."

...turned black and red.

She's a Ghost!

Rain reached for his rifle and fired Bullet Magic at her. He got off two shots, but the woman easily avoided both. However, his attack didn't end there...

They'll rebound!

Rain's Pharel bullets attacked the girl from behind, taking her by surprise—

"Oh."

—or so he'd thought, but the girl nimbly avoided them. She'd made that look far too easy, as if she had eyes in the back of her head.

"Phantasmal Bullets, eh...? This is the first time I've seen someone use it in battle."

"Ugh..."

Her cold voice sent shivers down Rain's spine. And then the girl pulled out a pistol before Rain's Qualia could predict it. He'd failed to even register her malicious intent.

Click!

"Good-bye."

The crimson girl shot Rain through his right eye.

Splat!

"Gaaah, aaaaaah!"

His right eyeball split into fragments of flesh and fluid with an almost comical sound.

Rain's consciousness started to fade, but he could still make out sounds around him.

"You poor thing. You shouldn't have gotten yourself involved with the Ghosts."

And that noble, dignified voice froze the blood running through his veins.

7. GHOST "KIRLILITH"

One hundred years.

It had been a full century since her execution. She'd awakened several times over the course of that century, but that only amounted to about two years in total, and her body hadn't matured at all.

And within that time, she'd met *him*, a boy who'd tried to fulfill her wish. He'd shared her hatred, the loathing she'd harbored after being executed for a crime she hadn't committed, and he'd erased countless people off the face of the earth for her.

But right now, that boy...

"I see."

...was dead. His limp body was at her feet, missing its right eye. A single glance was enough to tell he'd suffered a fatal injury. However, when Air stepped forward...

"Ah..."

...the boy's body leaped up. His upper half jumped as if on a spring, reaching out to grab her, but Air spotted that clumsy attack and moved back, easily avoiding his arm.

There was a huge gap in ability between a Ghost like her and this normal boy. So she was confident that no matter what he tried, he'd fail to even touch her. She'd handled him with surprising ease during the bullet royal, not taking a single blow, because of her superior strength.

But the next moment—

"What?!"

I can't get away!

An ominous premonition assailed her. And before Air could even take any evasive measures, the boy slammed her down against the ground.

"Urk, ah!"

Every bone in her body screeched, but before her consciousness shut down from the pain, his palm pressed against her neck.

"Ugh, aaah…"

The boy started strangling her with unnatural strength. Her vertebrae creaked.

"O-oh…"

But even as she was being strangled to death, Air shifted her gaze to the boy…

"So that's…what's going on…"

…to Rain's *right eye*.

"Now I know…what felt so off about you."

"…Yeah, I guess you do."

Rain no longer seemed to be on the verge of death. His right hand gripped Air's neck tightly, while his left wiped the blood from his eye. The fabric of his shirt was covering his eye socket, but it still remained visible.

"Though honestly, I didn't think I'd become such a monster."

His eyeball swiftly regenerated, turning *black and red*.

"Well, go figure."

Air smiled faintly, looking truly happy for the first time since she'd met Rain.

"You're just like me."

"Guess so. But I can't say I expected it to grow right back."

The boy's right eye had turned black and red, a combination of colors he'd seen several times over the last few days. The colors signaled the use of a unique brand of magic.

"It's nice to meet you, Ghost Rain Lantz."

Rain's right eye had regenerated, which tipped Air off to the truth.

"I can tell from our scuffle just now. Yours is the Ema divinity, which belonged to the Lupines... Wow, I didn't think it still existed."

"The Lupines..."

Air was still against the ground, her neck in Rain's grip. If the boy truly wished to strangle her, he could do so with little effort. The balance of power was firmly in his favor, but Air didn't falter.

"You didn't know?"

"The eye was implanted in me against my will. I never learned where it came from."

"Against your will?"

"Mm-hmm... Listen, I'm no Ghost. I haven't died yet. And... originally, I wasn't even a mage. I was just an ordinary human being, born without any capacity for magic," Rain said. But his eye proved that he'd gained the divinity of the Ema, the race said to be closest to God.

"Then you're..."

"Yeah," Rain answered, exposing the secret he'd kept hidden for so long. "I'm an artificial mage."

"Hmm... But still, to think you were given the same power *we* were."

"Yeah, it's weird. Normally, the quality of a mage's Qualia and mana are decided at birth, but everything changed once this artificial eye was implanted in me."

"I finally understand... The Ema's divinity is fixation of events... It's on a whole different level from the future sight mages employ. You don't predict the future—you *ascertain* it. Anything you see comes true without exception, making battle trivial."

In other words, it was a power that let Rain create the future he saw, which explained how he'd easily captured Air despite their difference in strength.

The Ema's eye activated over an extremely limited space and time, so the future it could ascertain was less than half a second ahead. But that was still more than enough; the briefest of movements controlled life and death in a battle.

"Who gave it to you?"

"...The West."

Rain spoke between ragged breaths as his ability unconsciously activated.

"For the first ten years of my life, I lived in a town called Luno. It was the closest town to the border."

Rain had decided to share his darkest memories with her.

"But seven years ago, it became a battlefield. And once the massacre ended, the remaining residents were rounded up and used as test subjects. They were trying to figure out if any of us were compatible with this eye, apparently."

Air's brow furrowed when she heard Rain's explanation.

"...They tried implanting divinity into human beings with no aptitude for magic?"

"I know. Insane, right? There was no reason for them to think it'd ever work, but..."

He held his breath for a long moment as he reached that part of the story.

"...the eye stayed in the hundredth person."

"Hmm..."

Rain still vividly recalled that particular sequence of events. They'd used magic to implant the artificial eye in him, and then, after a night of hellish pain and visions of the other ninety-nine people dying, he was found compatible...

"I see. So is that eye the source of your grudge?"

"Not exactly."

Rain hated the West, but not because of anything he'd said already.

"In a way, I'm glad I got this eye. I always wanted to be a mage, so it helped make my dream come true. But...I'll never forget what happened to my family."

Rain's expression never changed as he continued to speak of his depressing memories.

"I still remember their faces... I still remember *exactly* what happened when this eye rejected them. See, the moment it's implanted in someone, it begins to eat away at them. And if they succumb to its power, their entire body burns and disintegrates. It's a horrifically painful death. On that day, I saw my family, my friends... I saw everyone I ever loved get consumed by this eye, one by one."

When the East had eventually arrived to recover the bodies, they'd shuddered at the ghastly sight. Rain had seen mountains of corpses countless times in his life, but that was the one time they'd barely resembled human beings.

And that sight had stoked the dark flames of revenge that burned within his heart.

"My only goal in life is to find the person responsible for that atrocity and kill them. That's why I became a cadet at Alestra Academy."

The blood clots finally cleared from his eye, ruptured bones and skin mending as it returned to normal.

The flickering flames reflected in his eyes. The very same flames that had appeared in this brand-new world.

"Tell me everything."

"Wh-what do you…? Eek!"

"This isn't a threat."

Rain still had Air by the back of her neck, so he pushed her against the ground and stuck the muzzle of his gun against her brow. They were only a few inches apart, and she'd been rendered immobile. Air may have been a skilled mage, but it was impossible to avoid a shot from such a close distance.

"Hmm…"

She likely understood the situation. Air eyed the muzzle of his gun coldly, a smirk on her face. Rain, on the other hand, was determined to settle everything right then and there, so he'd had enough of her arrogant attitude.

I'm at my limit here…

He'd been waiting for a chance to pin Air down and squeeze more information out of her. And it'd taken a great deal of planning and resolve to get that far, so he was ready to shoot her dead if she resisted.

Unfortunately, it seemed his rather evident murderous intent wasn't enough. The girl remained undaunted as she said, "I see you've grown a backbone."

Her composure hadn't cracked one bit.

"…Tell me everything you know."

A strong breeze blew through the burning city as he made that demand and pressed the gun into her with renewed force.

"I don't have enough information to understand all the illogical things that've been happening around me. And I know I won't survive if I keep running around like a headless chicken."

"And if I say no?"

The sound of a gunshot boomed through the air. Smoke trailed up from Rain's gun as the blast rattled their eardrums.

"Eek...!"

"I'll start with your limbs...and keep going until you cooperate."

The bullet had shot off a bit of her lush, silver hair, and Air grimaced. The beautiful strands danced through the wind, glittering faintly in the moonlight.

"...Fine, I suppose I owe you some answers."

Air nodded, finally agreeing to talk. Apparently, she'd given in to Rain's demands. At her attitude, Rain decided to start with the most pressing question on his mind.

"What happened? How'd things end up worse?"

The world had shifted, so why had even more people died? His remaining classmates had even told him that most of their friends were dead.

"The Ghost, Kirlilith," Air said, then paused for a moment and added, "She manipulated Alec like a puppet and hid behind him. It seems like she's the true mastermind behind these attacks."

"...Kirlilith."

A girl who personified destruction, a being of pure red who contrasted Air's silver.

Kirlilith... Rain remembered her vividly. She was the girl who'd shot out his right eye.

"This isn't just about Alec. Kirlilith mentioned your name."

"Yes, I figured she would," Air admitted with a blank look on her face.

"So you really do know them?"

"Yes. I've known Alec for quite a while."

"Erase Alec..." Air had already known Alec was a Ghost when she'd given Rain that order. And yet, she'd still wanted him gone.

"...Are they both dead people, like you?"

"Yes."

Her answer was brief.

"There are several Ghosts in this world. They creep into each nation's military and leech off the currents of history like parasites. This time, Alec got in my way, so I had him removed. We'd been at each other's throats for seventy years, so that was a long time coming."

"Wait, slow down!"

Rain had started to lose track. Nothing about the Ghosts made any sense to him.

"What are Ghosts? You mentioned battling Alec over the last seventy years, so does that mean you revive every time a war breaks out to continue your fight?"

"That's right."

"But why? What for?"

"I've told you already, I don't know."

Air presented the black shell dangling from her neck to emphasize her point.

"All Ghosts have their existences sealed into black bullets like this one. But we don't know who's responsible for that practice or even who's managing this entire affair. But what's clear is that whenever a large-scale war breaks out, we Ghosts are brought into existence through these bullets. And..."

She paused there, unsure whether to tell him more.

"Everything ends once we die. There's no second resurrection."

"...Seriously?"

She doesn't know why, but she has to keep fighting through the ages?

"So why are you fighting each other? You don't hold some personal grudge against Alec or Kirlilith, do you?"

"Do you gun down enemy soldiers because of some personal grudge?"

"That's different."

"No, it's really not."

Her answer rang cruelly in his ears, but Rain knew she was telling the truth.

"You've heard my story already, so I'm sure you understand. Alec was a renowned soldier from the first war who was assassinated during an insurrection. And the rest of the Ghosts I've met are much like him and me..."

Air paused at that point and rolled up her sleeve before continuing her speech.

"All of them are war heroes who've gained this mark in death, along with the power of the corresponding Divine Sentinel."

She'd exposed the Belial's mark on her flesh, the proof of Air's inhuman power...

"There aren't that many out there, but I've seen the Traxil's, the Rentogral's, and the Achiral's specialized powers... Plus, you just experienced Alec's Oud ability, right?"

Alec's power had been most unusual. He'd had a bullet that let him control anything, even inanimate objects.

"I think I understand all that now, so let's get back to my first question."

Rain changed the subject to get the answer to his most pressing question.

"Why did everything turn out worse after the world shifted?"

The battle should've ended with Alec's disappearance, so what had gone wrong?

"It's simple, really. The Crimson Ghost, Kirlilith, set up all this ahead of time."

"Wait, what? How?"

"Alec was bait. She assumed they would run into trouble, so she set him up to take the fall. That's the best explanation I can come up with."

She'd assumed Alec would die...? She'd actually used an exemplary commander with unrivaled powers as mere bait?

"It just goes to show that Kirlilith is exceptional, even among Ghosts."

"Wait, that makes no sense. This only started *after* I erased Alec..."

"Well, what if she predicted that the Devil's Bullet would wipe Alec out of existence?"

Rain shuddered at the thought.

"And so here we are. We only met once, forty years ago, but she's a true monster who's lived as a Ghost for one hundred and fifty years now. I don't doubt that she's learned about my Devil's Bullet's abilities after fighting for so long."

That meant Kirlilith had inferred the Devil's Bullet's ability and worked around it?

But that's insane...

"It's clear she used Alec to lure me out."

Is that...even possible?

Letting Alec take command while assuming he'd be erased, pretending to be at a disadvantage, and then turning the tables once history had been rewritten to gain the upper hand... How could someone have planned and executed that so flawlessly?

"In chess terms, she allowed her pawn to be captured in order to clear a path for her queen to checkmate the enemy king. With Alec's disappearance, a unit that'd previously been left behind switched to the front lines. The crimson flames burning this town to ashes prove that."

The fire that was raging around them wasn't a normal blaze. It scorched everything in its path without wavering even once.

"Hers is the Traxil divinity, a bullet that invokes death."

"Death..."

"Yes. Kirlilith's divinity imbues her bullets with the ability to inflict death upon anything they hit. My bullets only affect humans, but that's because they're tied to the concept of history. Kirlilith's bullets, however, inflict death on an atomic scale. Anything they strike, human or otherwise, is utterly annihilated. Ever since she first revived as a Ghost, Kirlilith has slain tens of thousands of people with that power, drowning cities in flames, just like you see now."

Air's face didn't betray any hint of emotion as she told him all that, which spoke to the number of times she'd face similar horrors... It was a unique, unusual state of mind that all Ghosts shared. They'd long since accepted the necessity of having to kill other Ghosts and spill innocent blood, even if they despised such acts.

They'd repeated that process over and over and over again... and Air was no different.

"Rain."

Rain turned his eyes back to Air when he heard her say his name. Her gaze had retained its intensity even though he had her pinned; she stared straight at him as her eyes glinted sharply in an attempt to read him.

"Your feelings are absurdly misplaced."

"That's…"

Air had seen right through him. She'd realized a sense of sympathy, of misguided pity, had taken up residence within Rain's heart.

"I lost the right to be pitied the moment I was placed in this body."

"…Placed?"

"Yes," Air said before going quiet for several moments.

"I suppose this is as good a chance as any. How do I explain this…? Well, I suppose I already told you once, actually. This body may have been shaped according to Air Arland Noah's soul, but originally, it was someone else's. I'm simply parasitically inhabiting this shell."

As she said that, Rain realized that the hand he had around her neck was shaking. He hadn't noticed earlier, but Rain had been touching the *silver chain* of Air's black bullet the whole time.

This is…

His memories ached, releasing something that'd sunk into the depths of his consciousness. Something that had surfaced countless times in his dreams, only for him to seal it away.

A silver chain… A beautiful necklace… It was the first thing Rain had ever bought for *her*…

It can't be…

"Do you remember what I told you once?"

Air ignored Rain's confusion and continued her explanation.

"Whoever made the Ghosts has a bullet that can seal souls. And the owner of that bullet found worthy individuals, sealed their souls into black bullets like this one, and placed them inside other people's bodies. The mind of those hosts is then taken over... and their body morphs into the shape of the Ghost's soul as the container for a new life. We Ghosts have used many people as hosts throughout the ages."

Air was no exception; she'd been inhabiting a body she'd gained during the fourth war for as long as Rain had known her.

A *certain someone's* body...

"Are you still listening?"

Her words snapped Rain out of his thoughts.

"Look, when they implanted that eye in you, you saw countless deaths. You saw the blood of the innocent, the way that inferno even those who begged on their hands and knees. And that ignited the black flames in your heart, didn't it?"

Rain's desire for revenge didn't stem from himself, since he was alive and well. The rage burning inside him was a result of someone else's death...

"This body's former owner was...Rilm Lantz."

The name hit him like a kick in the chest.

Rilm Lantz—that made it all clear. What Air was, how she'd come to be...and the hatred festering within him.

"My body was once your younger sister's."

Air had said it. Her body had originally belonged to Rain's sister, Rilm Lantz.

"Ah...!"

Rain was in a stupor, and yet...

"You don't believe me, do you?"

...Air remained unperturbed.

"But there's no doubt in my mind. After all, some of her memories still linger in this shell. Its original name was Rilm Lantz. She was a perfectly ordinary eight-year-old child, born and raised in O'ltmenia."

She was the youngest child of the Lantz family, as well as their first daughter, Rilm Lantz. And seven years ago, during that battle in the city...her older brother had watched her die.

The West had launched a raid and taken the citizens hostage. Rain, who was at that point a completely ordinary ten-year-old child, was one of their victims.

They destroyed the town, killed 30 percent of its residents, and dragged the rest off without any rhyme or reason. The soldiers took Rain to an isolated large white facility. Over a hundred people were stuffed into one small room. He'd heard the men call it the "rat cage," and the prisoners were certainly treated as such.

Every few hours, soldiers appeared and picked five people at random. Their cuffs were unlocked, and they were taken outside with a gun shoved to their backs, never to be seen again. Anyone who resisted was shot on the spot. Their corpses were left where they fell, and after the third one, everyone stopped resisting.

After a few days, only the children remained. They had no way of knowing what had truly happened, but they assumed that everyone who'd been taken had died.

And then came that day...the final day.

Rain and Rilm were still in that room. They'd been watching the people they knew disappear to become corpses for several days now, and they'd seen their remains being carried off countless times, as well. They were the ones who'd been unable to withstand the divinity implanted in them, whose psyches had snapped from the unbearable pain.

And yet...Rilm never once cried.

She shivered in terror within that cramped room, but she simply clung to Rain and withstood it, refusing to cast aside the last thing she had—her pride.

He'd only just bought her that pendant...but she'd hung it on a silver chain that had just a bit of alloy mixed into it, and she clasped it tightly in her small hands, refusing to let her heart break under the pressure of all this violence.

He wanted to stay by her side. As Rilm's brother, he'd resolved to struggle against death alongside her. But when his turn came, the West's soldiers tore them apart. And without her brother to hold on to, Rilm was left truly alone... That was when she finally cried.

That was the last time he saw her alive. He'd only accepted her death when he later saw the mountain of corpses being transported away. They were all people who'd been in the room with Rain. And when he looked through it, he found the remains of the children as well.

"Only one person from that room survived, boy...," one of Rain's western guards had said. "You."

"And he lied to you," Air proclaimed. According to her, she'd risen from the grave after her death a hundred years ago, and she now inhabited Rilm's body...

"Only a few people from that room were transported to the West. Four, to be exact. And Rilm Lantz was one of them... It just so happens that I claimed her body."

"Don't fuck with me!" Rain had barely managed to keep himself in check. "You stole her body? That's impossible. You two have nothing in common. She had auburn hair. She looked nothing like you."

"None of that matters. Rilm's body was mere fodder."

Air's tone was perfectly even, as if she were just talking about the weather.

"…!"

And Rain lost all control of his emotions. He'd tried to understand her situation, but it had all been pointless. He loomed over Air and activated his Bullet Magic, unleashing it into her body.

"Aaah, ow…!"

He hadn't hit her directly, since the bullet had discharged next to her face, but a blast of electricity drilled into her all the same.

"Aaaaaah, gaaah…"

He'd tried to curb its effects, but the spell's primary use was to kill multiple people in one shot, so even a weak version hurt. The current running through her body peeled off her skin as white smoke rose from the wounds.

Rain wasn't spared any of that pain, either, since he was so close to her, but…

"Answer me."

…he didn't budge.

"How do I get you out of Rilm's body?"

"You can't— Ah, aaah!"

He attacked her again. Air's body jerked from the electrical current, spreading a charred stench around them.

"Ha-ha, ha-ha-ha…"

"Ugh… There has to be some way. Just tell me the truth!"

Air answered Rain's question with weak laughter; she didn't

waver even under heat strong enough to reduce her to ash. Rain increased the output and fired off a third attack, yet Air didn't tremble in the slightest.

A fourth followed. Then a fifth, a sixth, a seventh, an eighth, and eventually...

"Ugh..."

...Rain had exhausted his mana reserves. His artificial eye had turned black and red like a Ghost's, and a hot current circulated through his body.

Rilm...

Fury.

Regret.

His seething emotions dominated his consciousness, painting the world red. And they were all directed at one person. However—

"You can't...because Rilm Lantz is dead."

"Ah!"

Her answer was blunt and concise.

"She passed away before I was placed into this body. Immediately after the West took Rilm, they tried implanting an artificial eye in her, which ended in failure. And then my soul entered her body, where I slept until I met you."

The person Rain had sworn to protect, even at the cost of his life, was here before him. He'd lost her once because of his weakness, and now she'd returned—but it was wrong. It was all wrong.

He'd once watched his family get butchered. But now he knew that his sister, the one who'd suffered the most gruesome fate of all, had become the host of Air Arland Noah's soul...

......

How exactly was he supposed to accept all that?

"Listen, you didn't pick up those silver bullets by accident. I needed a person driven by hatred, and Rilm's memories revealed the most driven, most tenacious individual out there. That was how I knew you'd have a heart strong enough to use my Devil's Bullet, to erase people's existence without batting an eye."

Air had known what motivated him all along. She knew why he wished to use the Devil's Bullet. His lofty goal of ending the war hid his true desire—a simple, common desire to reclaim what he'd lost.

"You want to kill one specific person with the Devil's Bullet."

The person behind his family's death. Rain wanted to find the one responsible for the attack on his town, kill them with the Devil's Bullet, and shift the world to a state in which they'd never even existed.

"You believe that will bring back your family, don't you?"

"...No, I don't."

"You think it'll fix everything that's been broken."

"No."

"You've killed countless people, all for that naive desire."

"That's not true! I..." Rain tried to keep talking, but the rest of the words got stuck in his throat. He knew anything more would've just made him look like a child throwing a tantrum.

I... I'm...

Rain had fought countless battles, waded through raging infernos that reeked of blood and gunpowder. And the only thing that kept his sanity intact through all that pain, the only thing that justified all his actions, was the superficial excuse he'd repeated in his heart.

I'll end this war for good!

He'd convinced himself his actions were the only way to end the cycle of sorrow, but...

"Don't kid yourself, Rain. Ending the war is nothing more than a justification for your actions. Your only real wish is to bring back the sister you failed to protect."

If Rain found the person responsible for ruining his childhood and used the Devil's Bullet on him, the world would shift. Then, his hometown and family would never have been put to the torch. He'd never have spent time on a battlefield at all. And that was the actual reason Rain had erased so many soldiers from the West.

Air had called him out on his subconscious thoughts, merely fueling Rain's anger and fury. But as much as he wanted to deny her words, he couldn't. At his very core, he was too obsessed with revenge. Rain's sole reason for standing on the battlefield, his one and only wish, had been to avenge his friends and family, but that had changed with the introduction of the Devil's Bullet. However—

"It's impossible."

Air, the one who knew the Devil's Bullet best, rejected his subconscious desire.

"…Why? Theoretically speaking, it's *definitely* possible."

"Maybe, but it'll never happen. I'm not sure why, but in exchange for its power, the Devil's Bullet invokes a curse on its owner." Her hands curled, her fingernails digging into the fabric of her shirt. "The Devil's Bullet will never grant you what you desire most."

Air tore her thin clothing apart and exposed her upper body. If it hadn't been for the tense situation, Rain would've flinched, just as he had when she'd flipped up her skirt.

"That's…"

He was shocked by the sight of Air Arland Noah's exposed body—

"You see, these are all the scars I've gained during my battles as a Ghost."

Her body was laced with the markings of deep wounds. There were lacerations and burn marks everywhere, and Rain thought he saw many gunshot wounds as well. They were all far too ghastly, far too gruesome on the soft white flesh of a beautiful girl.

A wave of nausea struck Rain.

"These aren't Rilm's scars. They're mine. And even when I erased the people who wounded me, the scars never faded. They are my mark of shame."

That was the curse of the Devil's Bullet. It would never grant the user's true wish, including Air's wish to wipe her scars away.

All she wanted was to obtain a perfect, unblemished body, a desire that spoke to the brutal life she'd lived on the battlefield.

"…Enough."

"Mmm? Enchanted, are you— Bwah!"

"Quit teasing me and put this on. I get what you're trying to say, okay?"

Rain rose to his knees and finally removed his weight from her. And as he stood up, he took off his uniform's jacket and dumped it over her, unintentionally lowering the barrel of his gun.

This…is a Ghost.

But he didn't lift it up again. He'd finally realized why Air always freaked out when someone tried to touch her. The reason she'd knocked Rain down to the ground and nearly killed a fellow classmate was because she hated her own body.

…Goddammit!

Her soul had been imprisoned in another person's corpse, and she was covered in grisly scars that served as the sole proof of the life she'd lived.

How could someone have lived such a tragic life?

She'd failed to gain true peace even in death, because someone had bound her soul and placed it in another person's body and forced her back onto the battlefield.

"Well, let's just put all that aside for now and get to the matter at hand." Air seemed to want to change topics. "I know how much you despise them, but it's not enough. Among the Ghosts, Kirlilith is on a whole different level. She's a true genius!"

"...I see."

"Also, thanks for the clothes." Air finished putting on his jacket, then flapped its sleeves. "I don't really like showing them to people."

"Then don't."

"But your reactions are so funny. They honestly make me want to tease you more."

Rain couldn't tell whether she truly meant those words, but either way, he didn't have the time to ask. As he gazed at her, Air flicked her silver hair back with her hand and said, "Kirlilith's here to kill me. The real battle will soon begin."

Air looked up at the moonlit sky shortly after. Something in her expression was tragically charged with emotion, as if she herself was as transient as the moon.

The train they were on had reached Alestra Academy at last.

The classroom felt empty with most of Rain's classmates gone.

So many of them died...

None of the survivors even spoke between their scheduled lectures.

It'd been three days since the attack on Leminus...and neither their physical wounds nor their emotional ones had healed.

It'll be fine…

Rain clutched the silver bullet in his hand.

So long as I have this… So long as I use it correctly…

The Devil's Bullet was his ticket out of the dark situation.

I'll use this to erase Kirlilith, the Ghost who killed them.

That was all he had to do. That was all that needed to happen. Alec had served as proof that even Ghosts weren't immune to Reprogramming. And Air seemed confident that only Kirlilith could've cooked up such a vile scheme.

Rain knew he could change everything by wiping her from existence. It was the only way to restore Leminus and save all his classmates.

Throb, throb—his regenerated right eye had been beating like a heart in his skull, but with every pulse came pain.

The Ema, huh…?

Air had informed Rain that the cursed power in his right eye was the ability of one of the Ghosts. In other words, the very thing that made him a mage also allowed him to stand on equal ground with Kirlilith.

It'll be fine. I can do it… No, I have to do it.

"Hey, Rain," Orca called out to him, breaking the dull silence. "Athly isn't back yet, is she?"

"…No, she isn't," Rain replied weakly. Then he added, "Her parents just got killed, so classes are the least of her worries."

Orca lowered his head forlornly and returned to his seat.

Days later, the cadets were sent out to another battlefield.

They'd been deployed to a mine that was half a day's drive away from Alestra Academy.

It was a graimar-nuclear-alloy vein, essential for Exelia production, so the two countries often fought over possession of the resource. This was one of those contested areas.

The location's official designation was the Claw Mine.

The East's main forces had gathered there, forming a large military presence. However, the battle still reached the cadets rather quickly. By the time they'd arrived, the two sides had already been engaged in battle for three hours.

The Claw Mine had been scorched by fire Bullet Magic, and the rear base had gradually filled with mangled bodies and wounded soldiers missing limbs. The living were hard to distinguish from the dead at this point.

The cadets hadn't been deployed to the front lines yet, but they knew that wouldn't last much longer. The East's army was getting desperate.

Kirlilith's command of the West's forces had dictated every aspect of the battle thus far, so their backs were to the wall.

"You're sure, Air? That the enemy commander is Kirlilith, I mean."

"Yes. I have proof."

Air sat next to Rain as they remained on standby in the Exelia hangar.

"The battle over this mine is her way of challenging me. With thousands of others caught in the cross fire."

She had the audacity to risk so many lives just to face a rival Ghost?

"Every Ghost has a distorted set of values. We've fought through countless major battles over the ages and have gained knowledge that normal humans can't hope to obtain as a result. I doubt Kirlilith would pick a fight with me in any old ordinary clash."

I see. That's...

"It's disgusting."

"It sure is. And that's why we have to kill her right here, right now."

Rain didn't speak to Air after that. She was deep in thought, trying to figure out how to gun down Kirlilith, so he didn't want to interrupt her. He knew there was nothing he could've said to help her anyway, since his human intellect was no match for hers.

"...I'll step out for a bit."

Rain left her alone and walked to the adjacent hangar.

And there he found Athly, who'd been performing maintenance on her unit. She quickly noticed him.

"Huh? Is it time to change shifts already?" Athly asked him curtly. It was an unnatural reaction coming from her, since she was usually such a cheerful person.

"No, you've still got an hour left."

"Oh..."

She never lifted her eyes off her machine as she spoke. She was just one of the many people had been adversely affected by the last shift in the world.

"Say, shouldn't you stay off the battlefield for a while?"

"Why?"

"You know why."

"My parents' death doesn't change anything."

The Reprogramming had put Athly's parents among the thousands of victims in Leminus. A shell had hit their shelter, blowing them to bits. And it was all Rain and his silver bullet's fault.

"I'm fine, really," Athly stated in a monotone voice. "Like, I'm sorry if this sounds kind of rude, but it hasn't really affected me at all."

"It hasn't?"

"Yeah. Honestly, it's changed so little that it feels weird."

"Weird how…?"

"I mean, Mom and Dad were much stronger mages than me," Athly said as she pulled out the gun holstered at her waist. "I figured I'd never match them, even though I shared their genes. That's why I chose to become a manipulator in the first place. But then they died. Just like that, they were gone. And that made me realize something… A person's potential doesn't matter if they die in battle."

"…Athly."

"So I'm fine. I can jump into those flames…into the blood and the smoke, and I never have to worry."

Nothing she'd said made any sense. The words themselves were clear, but they didn't connect to form a cohesive point.

Rain knew they were the weak excuses of an emotionally wounded individual.

"...Listen, Athly. If you need anything, just say the word."

"Sure."

Unfortunately, that was why he couldn't bring himself to push her any further, and could offer her nothing more than a vague offer of support. And then they went their separate ways.

Rain should've done more to keep Athly out of that battle, but by the time he realized that, it was far too late for regrets.

Three hours after the start of the battle, the two sides were in a deadlock.

`"I'm so happy."`

Someone was speaking through a wireless line that connected the thirty or so commanders among the East's main forces.

`"You came for me... You really are amazing, Air."`

And the one speaking was Kirlilith. She cleared her throat and began speaking in an official capacity.

`"Ahem... Now then, people of the East... Fifteen minutes from now, we will blow up the Claw Mine."`

Blow up the mine...? Everyone from the East froze upon hearing the threat.

`"I'm sure you're all aware, but in its raw form, graimar nuclear alloy is extremely flammable and combustible. Exposing it to high heat will produce artificial plasma that will induce a series of explosions and destroy the mine. Quite bothersome, wouldn't you say? After all, this is your prime source of alloy."`

Kirlilith was as casual as could be about this.

`"If you wish to avoid that fate, surrender Air to me."`

Air...

"Do that, and we will cease all hostilities and retreat immediately."

None of the commanding officers knew who Air was. Her existence as a Ghost hadn't been disclosed to the public, so they likely assumed it was some sort of code.

"Now, allow me to demonstrate that this is no mere threat."

The next moment, a light flashed in the distance.

"Holy...!"

A second later, a pillar of fire rose up from an abandoned mine to the south, razing the place to the ground. It'd been only a fifth of the Claw Mine in size, but it was by no means a small site. Yet that entire mountain...had been reduced to rubble.

Kirlilith's crimson flames coiled upward, painting the dark sky red and striking fear into the hearts of all who saw them.

"Please hand Air over to me immediately. You have ten minutes. If I don't get a satisfactory response by then, I'll blow the Claw Mine sky-high."

"I knew all this was about me..."

Air scratched her hair roughly in frustration and threw aside the device she and Rain been using to tap into the commanders' communication line.

"She's insane."

"What do we do?"

They couldn't let Kirlilith blow up the Claw Mine. Without the alloy harvested there, the East would be forced into a bitter war with a hopeless deficit in resources. They knew HQ would seek Air out in order to meet Kirlilith's demands; she'd already proved blowing up the mine was not an idle threat.

"I can't show my face."

"...What, you afraid of getting sacrificed?"

"No. Weren't you listening?"

"Of course I was. Kirlilith said to hand you over."

"Don't take what she said at face value. Think about it. Why? Why did Kirlilith make handing me over the condition? Do you really think she'd surrender the mine and retreat in exchange for one person? It doesn't add up."

Air was right—it didn't add up. Trading one person for a prime source of alloy made no sense.

"Maybe it'd make sense if it was some famous officer, but no one knows who I am. The people at HQ are probably scrambling to find me, but Kirlilith doesn't intend to fulfill her end of the bargain. I mean, sure, she's got some clout in the West, but she's still just one person in the chain of command. She can't mobilize an army for personal matters."

In other words...

"She's going to blow up the Claw Mine regardless of what we do," Air explained.

"But what about her conditions?"

"She lied." Air had read Kirlilith's true intentions. "You're probably wondering why she even bothered to bring it up in that case, right? Well, the answer to that question lies with Kirlilith's unique magic."

Kirlilith had the Traxil's divinity, which granted her bullets the ability to inflict death on anyone and anything they hit. It was optimized for offense, unrivaled by any regular Bullet Magic, and it also gave her the power to destroy the Claw Mine.

According to Air, Kirlilith's bullets could easily collapse rocks and stones. They didn't just mow things down with heat or mass.

Instead, anything they touched died because it was destroyed on an atomic level.

"Yes. And she said they needed significant heat to blow up the mine, correct?"

"Which means..." Rain trailed off as he got lost in thought. Then he said, "Honestly, I dunno."

"It means Kirlilith is in charge of blowing up the mine," Air replied, exasperated. "Kirlilith probably struck some sort of deal with her army. 'I'll blow up the mine for you, so let me talk with the enemy for a bit. Oh, and don't worry—everything I say will be a lie.' Or something along those lines."

"Ah..."

"So do you understand why Kirlilith made that crazy demand?"

It didn't matter if her demands were crazy, since she didn't intend to keep her promise either way.

"...Wait, why'd she do that, then?"

It didn't make any sense. What was the point of bringing up a fake exchange?

"I told you at the beginning, didn't I? She's only after the other Ghost here—me."

Ghosts naturally sought out other Ghosts.

"In that short message, she dropped a number of hints. The first was that she'd blow up the mine regardless of the deal. The second was that she'd do it herself. Think about it—in order to use Bullet Magic to destroy the Claw Mine, she'll have to be *somewhere safe*, and at the same time, she'll need to aim at a *place packed full of alloy*."

In other words, Kirlilith was at a spot that met both those criteria...and she'd hid that fact in her little speech.

"She's trying to tell us *exactly* where she is."

She'd left a code, an encrypted message only Air would be able to decode.

"It was a challenge to me. 'I'll tell you where I am, so hurry over to kill me. If you don't, I'll blow up the Claw Mine.' Get it?"

After Air had laid out her explanation, Rain spread out a map of the mine and searched for a spot that fit the description. There was just one.

Reports were flooding in through her allied units. New information was arriving once every four seconds, and the one intercepting all of it was…

Aren't you coming?

…a beautiful girl who seemed to be made of flames. A crimson soul who had been killed by a stray bullet to the head one hundred and forty years ago while she was running through fire and brimstone.

Air…

Kirlilith Lambert. Despite her dainty, frail visage, she was the oldest and most cunning active Ghost, a veteran of countless battlefields. Of course she'd noticed them.

"Thank goodness. You're finally here," she said into the darkness.

Soon after, a mechanical sound whirred near her.

"That's a rather absurd thing to say when I'm here to end your life."

A lone silver girl had arrived in her Exelia, with a sharp glint in her eyes. No, she wasn't alone after all.

"How…? How are you still alive?"

Air's gunner had arrived alongside her—the boy Kirlilith had shot through the eye. She'd killed him because he knew of Air's existence, but he hadn't stayed dead.

"Can't say I wanted to face you again," he said as he trained his gun's sights on her. If she recalled correctly, that cadet's name was...Rain Lantz. "Personally, I hate to compare us, but you Ghosts aren't the only ones who don't stay down."

"A divinity? Or perhaps some kind of magic?" Kirlilith took a moment to ponder how the boy had survived, but she stopped soon after. It didn't really matter, and she had all the time in the world to figure it out once she killed him again.

"So why did you call me out here? Is there something you want to tell me?"

"Yes. It's very important... Listen, Air. Why don't we join forces?"

"Join forces...?" Kirlilith's words had caught Air entirely off guard. "...What, do you expect me to betray the East? Because if you are—"

"No, don't worry."

It was already late into the night. The moonlight was waning, but the flames flickered brightly, making the scenery around them as bright as at sunrise.

"I'm willing to defect, so will you accept me into the East?"

A beat of silence followed.

"Let's fight together, hand in hand."

They couldn't fathom what she was saying. Fight? Together?

"Have you lost it?"

"I'm not sure. Have I?"

"The East isn't in any sort of favorable position, Kirlilith.

You've supported Harborant for so long—what reason do you have to double-cross them now?"

"What reason? Well, you just said it yourself, Air. This time, the West is *too* strong. That's my only reason, really."

"What...?"

"The war will end at this rate."

It took Air a moment to realize what she was implying.

"Just think about it, Air. This war favors Harborant too heavily. That's not a good thing... After all, we Ghosts only exist during times of war."

Rain leaned toward Air and whispered, "Is that right?"

"Yeah. When the fighting dies down, our consciousness starts to fade. Next thing we know, we're in another war, decades later. It's happened to me several times already."

Apparently, they didn't know the logic behind how it worked. They couldn't tell whether someone was working the magic that tethered them behind the scenes or whether the spell itself simply had a time limit. Either way, a Ghost's existence was limited.

Once the war ended, all of them would disappear.

"So...what, you're saying you want to betray the West, Kirlilith?"

"Yes. I need the war to continue so that I can remain, too," Kirlilith said, sounding utterly desperate. "Over the past hundred years, I've led the West to countless victories. But this time, O'ltmenia is too weak... No, it's more that Harborant has grown too strong. Their advanced Exelias have superior mobility and durability, and they have Bullet Magic optimized for combat that almost anyone can use. They're stronger than the East in every conceivable way."

"Is that why you're gonna betray them?"

"Rain, be quiet."

"Sorry, but there's something I need to know."

Rain's interruption had bothered Air enough for her to chide him. But that didn't matter; he had the right to ask. After all, Kirlilith had orchestrated the massacre that had claimed the lives of dozens of his friends and comrades. But he couldn't forget this was war. Even if they had been students, they had been soldiers above that. They'd chosen to fight knowing they might die. If she was a murderer, then so were they. Venting his anger at her was pointless; all he really wanted to do was find out what drove her.

"Kirlilith, don't you feel anything for the West?"

"Feel...anything?"

"Yeah. How do you feel about the country you've been help-ing for over a hundred years?"

"How do I...feel?"

She looked up to the sky, seemingly confused by his question.

"Ha-ha-ha!" Kirlilith suddenly cackled. The grin on her face was lovely, yet terribly sad... "I've never once thought about that. In my eyes, wars and countries are but a means to live. A policy, a process...nothing more... Oh, I see. You're worried, aren't you? Well, don't be. I assure you that I will not hesitate to kill the peo-ple of the West. And if you need proof, I can call my forces over and blow them up along with the mine."

I'll show I can kill them...

She was ready and willing to sacrifice her own comrades, the very people who'd placed their trust in her.

And Rain finally realized the truth.

Oh, she's...empty.

Kirlilith was a void. She didn't have anything she wanted to protect or any sort of real purpose. She was just like a ghost from a storybook, acting to preserve her existence like a parasite. She had no friends or foes of any sort. She simply killed to suit her purposes.

"Join hands with me, Air. We can stay in this world for as long as we wish—we only have to use your bullet's ability to change history and my bullet's ability to invoke death. Let us fight, together, and prove that we exist!"

Her point was sound, but Air...

"Sorry, I'll pass."

...firmly rejected her.

"That sounds boring. I didn't think you'd be so pathetic, Kirlilith."

"...What?"

"Use my power to continue the war? Use my power, which has the potential to shake the very foundations of this world, just to prolong my existence and delay the inevitable?" Air mocked Kirlilith's suggestion as if it was the stupidest idea in the world. "Compared to your mind-numbingly dull invitation, this child's offer is far more interesting," Air said as she poked her thumb in Rain's direction.

"What...did he offer you?"

"He's trying to use my bullet's power to *end* the war." Air activated her Exelia as she said that. "And not just this war, either. He's going to use my power to overwhelm the West so thoroughly that no wars ever break out again. His wish to end all future conflict."

"That's..."

"Oh yes. Without war, we Ghosts will have no reason to exist. Plus, no one's ever been able to permanently end the fighting, so it's most likely impossible."

"In that case—"

"But it *is* interesting." Air cut off Kirlilith to bring an end to her pleas. "If nothing else, it's far more interesting than your ridiculous suggestion to keep fighting endlessly. This conversation is over, just like your existence as a Ghost."

"...I see. So be it, then."

Negotiations had concluded. After that, Kirlilith looked around with an icy gaze. After a few moments of hesitation, she lowered her head. When she raised it again, her eyes were dyed black and red.

"That means...!"

They were pitch-black, reflecting her unfathomable hatred. Those wasp-hued eyes were both proof of her identity as a Ghost and evidence of her malicious, murderous intent.

"Good-bye, then, Air. I will miss having one more Ghost to fight."

"Yes, farewell, Kirlilith. I'm sure you won't be so bored in the afterlife."

Their Qualia were honed to razor-sharp precision, marking the beginning of a battle between mages blessed with future sight.

Every Ghost, without exception, was armed with divinities that set them apart.

Ordinary Bullet Magic was akin to mass-produced weaponry, so it was easy to learn. But in the end, it was only a mock imitation of divinity. The Ghosts' magic used real divinity at its core, leading to the creation of higher-level phenomena.

"Horgo Bardas."

The moment the battle began, Kirlilith fired off a shot that turned into pure heat, swelling up to crush their surroundings. A single spell from her had created a deafening explosion, splitting the earth and scattering molten rock in all directions, and forming a stream of lava.

Crimson flames kicked up all around them.

She is way *stronger than any ordinary mage!*

Large-scale death and destruction bore down on them. Kirlilith had used a bullet that inflicted death on anyone it touched, so it spelled doom for any unfortunate soul it so much as clipped.

"Rain." Air uttered his name as she activated their Exelia. Rain braced himself as soon as he heard that, and in no time flat, their unit accelerated.

Ugh…

He withstood the inertia flinging him around inside the vehicle, but the very next moment, Air flipped them around and accelerated again.

If she keeps this up, I'll lose my lunch!

She operated the Exelia with such incredible speed that Rain struggled to keep up with the action.

"We can't let her control the flow of the battle. It's our turn now. Get ready to fire back," Air instructed as she avoided bullets from all directions.

She really isn't human!

A battle between mages depended almost entirely on Qualia. Whoever predicted their enemy's actions most accurately and swiftly came out on top. If one could use their future sight to react even milliseconds faster than their opponent, their bullet would hit first. Which meant...

What an...insane fight!

...their Qualia were equal. And if two mages were equally matched in terms of both Qualia and skill, the battle turned into a simple exchange of blows. Kirlilith deftly avoided shots Rain assumed would hit, and then, as soon as they stepped into what felt like a safe spot, her Bullet Magic was bearing down on them.

Their skirmish had begun only a few minutes ago, but they'd already exchanged thirty-odd blows. Honestly,

Rain couldn't help but be impressed. The two Ghosts had surpassed his wildest expectations.

Air had focused her Qualia on operating the Exelia, but Kirlilith had used hers to try to land a killing blow. The bullets that zoomed past them were charged with deadly heat, and when they crashed into the nearby ground, they created depressions that seemed like the work of a meteor shower.

The Belial and Traxil divinities, the bullet of Oblivion and the bullet of Death, clashed.

Each Exelia unit consisted of two people. Kirlilith served as the gunner, while her manipulator was some unknown western soldier. He'd been doing a fine job supporting her, but Rain knew he was the easiest target.

"Air…"

"Got it."

Air instantly realized his intent and shifted their Exelia's positioning. She changed her strategy, deciding to get into the best possible position to help Rain aim, instead of focusing on evasion, as she had so far.

"I'll place my faith in you."

Rain activated his utterly ordinary Bullet Magic…Pharel.

"Shoot, Rain!"

The moment Rain opened fire, their opponent dodged nimbly, evading a direct hit. But his bullet didn't stop there. If normal bullets were a point that extended like a spear, then Rain's bullets were a surface that spread out like a shock wave. The bullet that had initially missed its mark rebounded against a tree, striking the Exelia from the rear.

Boom!

It was a trick that surprised ordinary mages. The more experienced they were, the more unavoidable the bullet became. But...

How predictable.

...Kirlilith had seen right through it. Just before the bullet had struck, she'd fired a shot backward, hitting Rain's bullet with a feat of precise marksmanship akin to threading a needle.

I already know you use Pharel, so I can include it in my predictions...

Rain's magic fizzled out. The bullet itself broke apart and fell to the ground as scrap.

Your magic...won't work on me!

Once she confirmed she was safe, Kirlilith looked around to assess the situation.

No one, not a single person, will ever touch me!

Kirlilith's bullets affected everything equally. Anything they touched was annihilated, enemy Bullet Magic included. Even if her opponent far outclassed her when it came to Exelia combat—or even if they shot advanced, multilayered Bullet Magic at her—she would always be able to turn the tables on them with a single shot.

On top of that, she'd perceived the way his bullets rebounded. Pharel was already effectively useless when one expected it, but she'd even analyzed all the subtle movements of his bullets to make sure they'd never hit her. Long story short...

He's so weak...

...Kirlilith was disappointed. Their lack of strength had greatly disappointed her.

You're so weak*! What the hell?! Are you...really a Ghost like me?!*

Filled with rage, Kirlilith fired the Traxil's bullet. Air responded deftly, swerving her unit to easily avoid Kirlilith's attack. Her precise reactions exceeded human capabilities, proving that Air was indeed a Ghost. But that only made things worse.

No, Air! You weren't like this before! You were far more noble, far stronger, because you always fought alone! So why...? Why are you letting that child handle things?!

The boy's lack of strength was especially apparent when he was next to Air.

If you'd just used him as a pawn, you'd be so much stronger!

The rules of Exelia combat stated that all teams must be formed of pairs, but not once had Kirlilith ever treated the manipulator beside her as a partner. She'd bound the soul of the mage riding with her through the pact, controlling him to suit her needs.

And that was the natural order of things. Ghosts were at their strongest when they fought alone. That was why the magic of the pact existed. It was why all the Ghosts she'd encountered thus far had fought alone.

But that silver-haired girl didn't completely subjugate the boy. She did give him some instructions, but it seemed she fully entrusted the timing and power of the attacks to him. She hadn't been like that before. She had once treated her partners as slaves, just as Kirlilith did. She had abandoned her source of strength.

"......"

Unable to bear it any longer, she decided to address Air's unit through the megaphone.

"If you use the pact to control him and fight alone, you'll be so much stronger! You do know this, don't you? So long as you let that human handle the magic, you'll never beat me!"

No answer came. In place of a response, Bullet Magic fired in random directions from Air's unit.

Enough!

She knew those random shots would never hit her; they'd turned into an annoyance.

"That's enough. If you aren't going to put up a real fight, I'll just put an end to you!"

In an attempt to show Air the error of her ways, Kirlilith closed the gap between them and unleashed the Traxil's bullet of death. And one out of the seven shots she fired…

"Ah…!"

…hit Air's unit.

A violent impact jolted them.

"Ugh, aaah!"

Kirlilith's bullet had hit their Exelia's front section, blowing it apart. Luckily, they'd purged that leg right before the shot had landed. If they hadn't, their unit would've been reduced to scrap altogether.

"Ugh…"

That wasn't to say they got away unscathed, though. The after-shocks of the massive blast had definitely reached Rain and Air.

"A-Air…"

Rain's consciousness was hazy. Every part of his body screamed in pain. Kirlilith's bullet had sent their unit flying, and his body jostled and banged repeatedly until the unit eventually stopped tumbling at the bottom of the forested mountain. The only real silver lining was that they'd gotten out of Kirlilith's range.

"Hey… Air. Hurry, we've gotta move!"

Kirlilith would be here before long, so they were in as much danger as ever. Rain had called out to Air blindly, since his sight was still muddled, but Air had never fully ignored any of his requests before. He had no reason to worry...but her silence surprised him.

Rain gazed at her back, trying to focus his vision...and froze. "That wound..."

Red was everywhere. Blood was pouring from Air's right arm. "Haaah... Haaah..."

Air panted heavily, barely managing to stay conscious as she put pressure on her wounded arm with her healthy one. But upon realizing that it hadn't helped at all, she swiftly returned to operating the Exelia.

"Wait, you're too injured to do that!"

Rain reached out to grab her shoulder and stop her, since she was clearly in no condition to drive. But...

"Ow! Hey!"

"I'm fine."

...Air slapped Rain's arm away without even turning to face him. She'd rejected him.

Just like always, Air refused to let anyone touch her. "I'm fine. I can still fight... One of the Exelia's legs is missing, but it can still move."

Upon hearing that, Rain looked at the heavily damaged unit and replied, "There's no way that's true... You seriously think you can drive a damaged Exelia with one arm?"

"Well, what other options do we have?" Still breathing heavily, Air struggled to turn the Exelia on with her good arm. "We can't keep running. In this state, Kirlilith will *definitely* corner us. Our only way out of here is...through her..."

Wasn't there any way to win? Kirlilith had shown off the incredible advantage she had over them, so Rain knew a frontal assault wouldn't work. He couldn't overcome the difference in their skill, which meant he needed some other method of turning the tide. And as he started racking his brain, it dawned on him.

Earlier, didn't Kirlilith say...

"If you use the pact to control him and fight alone, you'll be so much stronger! You do know this, don't you?"

He'd never heard of any such thing before. Air had kept this little detail hidden from Rain thus far.

"Air."

"...What now?"

"Was what Kirlilith said earlier true?"

"Oh... Yeah," Air said, clearly still in a daze. "She's right... If I forcibly manipulated you, I'd be stronger for it. That much is fact."

"If that's the case..."

Why hadn't she done it already? Rain was a soldier who preferred to use the most logical, sound tactics available, and he knew Air was in the same boat, so this felt wrong.

I did think it was strange...

Air had demanded he enter a pact in exchange for the Devil's Bullet, but she hadn't actually ever used it to bypass his will. She may have verbally ordered him at times, but she'd never invoked the actual pact to force his hand. He'd always thought that it was simply because nothing they'd faced had required it, but he realized he was wrong.

Air had made a conscious decision not to use it, even in life-and-death situations. Kirlilith had mentioned the pact let a Ghost exhibit their full capabilities. They excelled at fighting solo, and manipulating others was a part of that.

"Why not use it?" he asked. "Shouldn't you control me with the pact in this fight?"

"...So what if it's the ideal solution?"

"What are you...?"

"Doing that has never"—Air hung her head and briefly paused before continuing—"changed anything."

Her voice was hoarse, and she wasn't at all her usual self. The wound had clearly muddled her consciousness and clouded her judgment. Still, that also meant she was being completely honest with him.

"Forcing you to do something is easy... I can even make you commit suicide if I want. But a person who's been forced to do something...will never truly forgive the one who coerced them."

Those words weren't directed at Rain; they were more of a warning for herself.

"The stronger your powers get, the lonelier you become... And magic that lets you command others is the most extreme example of that... All people who manipulate others to suit their own needs...end up in the same place. All alone."

They would find themselves in utter darkness, drowning in their own despair.

"I believed in them... I thought we had a special bond, but..."

Blasts of Kirlilith's long-range fire roared around them as Air spoke.

"I was...the only one who felt that way..." Air struggled to convey her true feelings, her voice little more than a whisper. "The moment I invoked the pact, I ended up alone."

She'd finally regained a bit of her strength now. Tightening her grip on the Exelia's steering wheel, she moved their three-legged unit to widen the gap between them and Kirlilith.

She's lonely...

Air had said that the world never truly changed. Even with the immense power of the Devil's Bullet in hand, she'd been unable to make a real difference.

......

Rain didn't know how much she'd suffered. He didn't know what she'd lost in exchange for her great power, or how she'd felt when people betrayed her... But...

"The moment I invoked the pact, I ended up alone."

...he'd caught a glimpse of the burden on her shoulders.

However, he didn't have the time to entertain such thoughts as Kirlilith's unit came into view in the distance.

"I'm just asking to be on the safe side, but it's not too late for you to start using the pact, right?"

"It's not impossible."

Luckily, Air seemed to have recovered enough to think of a plan.

"But our timing is bad... The rig's missing a leg, and I've only got one working arm."

"...So we've got no real chance, huh?"

"Pretty much."

He'd realized they were in a hopeless situation, but he still didn't intend to rush in and accept death. Rain wanted to act only if they had some small chance of success.

It'll come down to a gamble. If we get even the smallest chance, we have to bet on it...

However, the moment the word *gamble* rose to his mind, he thought of something.

"...Air, I might have a plan."

"Oh? What?"

"It's pretty risky..."

They had no realistic shot of winning, but that plan at least gave them a fighting chance. So Rain informed Air of his idea, then patiently awaited her response.

"You want to blindly fire off Pharels?"

"Right. Multiple shots, so many that even my future sight can't keep up, all over this thicket."

It was actually the simplest plan imaginable. He'd shoot at random and pray for a hit.

"Hmm, well... I suppose the probability you'll hit her isn't zero."

If Rain couldn't predict the trajectory of his bullet, then neither could Kirlilith. That meant the best strategy was to fire Pharels at random and bet on their luck.

At best, he'd hit Kirlilith. At worst, his own bullets would hit him. It was a literal gamble. But mages always employed methods with the highest probability of success, so this would throw Kirlilith off her game.

"...You think that relying on luck, on a reckless attack that could end up killing you instead, will fool Kirlilith because she relies on logic?"

"Exactly."

If they were going to gamble anyway, this was the best available option. After all, the bigger the risk, the greater the reward.

"Fine. We'll go with that."

Air eventually approved of his tactics. Shooting Pharels at random... The plan had an excessively low chance of success, but it was their only hope.

......

"Air."

"What? Do you have something else to add?"

Bam!

"Ouch!"

Rain whacked Air in the head with his gun. She'd already suffered a major injury, so the blow only made it worse.

"What was that for?!"

"How long are you gonna keep being so weak?"

"I'm not weak."

"Then how'd I manage to land that hit on you?"

"That's…"

Normally, Rain would never have managed to hit her, so he knew something was up.

"…I'll be honest. I can't really understand the baggage you're carrying. I can only try to imagine your reasons for not invoking the pact and why you said the world won't change."

Rain paused for a moment to gather his thoughts.

"But…we still have to change it."

"……"

"This isn't about who's right. When two sides that won't back down clash, one of them has to crumble."

There was no point discussing who was right and wrong, because neither was actually wrong. Both had sound arguments. But if battle was the only proper form of debate, the only way to figure out who deserved to come out on top, then they'd fight.

Rain fixed his grip on his rifle and held his breath. He was nervous, betting both their lives like this.

"You said you can't change the world…but I can. If everything around us is evil, then I'll change every last bit of it."

"…Ha-ha-ha," Air chuckled as she heard his bold proclamation. Then she replied, "You sure talk a big game for someone so naive… But sure, I'll humor you. Go on—show me what you can accomplish."

She fixed their unit's bearing, but it was no longer angled toward retreat…

"We'll gun down Kirlilith here and now. How hard could changing the world be, right?"

Instead, she'd aimed to intercept the Ghost charging at them.

Rain's strategy was fairly basic. He'd decided to shoot wildly in her general direction, which left him with a less than 50 percent chance of victory. In other words, he'd abandoned his abilities as a mage. He'd thrown aside his Qualia to create a weak spot in Kirlilith's future sight, meaning he was basically just praying the bullets hit. Kirlilith could still evade the bullets' trajectories, so their chances of success were slim, but this wager was their only hope of seeing tomorrow.

The enemy entered Rain's firing range.

I have twenty shots…

As Kirlilith's unit charged toward them, Rain activated his magic, unleashing all his mana-charged bullets at once.

Ugh…!

The bullets rebounded. Rain had unleashed his Bullet Magic, but he couldn't tell any of their trajectories.

Hit her…

The rebounding bullets flitted about before his eyes. He'd shot the bullets straight ahead, but a few of them rebounded back in their direction. Luckily, Air's superhuman reflexes allowed them to evade.

Hit her, dammit!

The results of their gamble soon became apparent.

"Ah…!"

A blast filled the air. Kirlilith's unit billowed black smoke from a few feet in front of them, scattering damaged parts into the air. And when Rain's remaining bullets dispersed, the threat disappeared with it.

"Haaah… Haaah…"

Rain's breath caught in his throat.

I...won?

Kirlilith's unit had been destroyed, so they'd come out on top. However, right when that thought crossed his mind—

"Ugh!"

`"Even an utterly idiotic plan can be...formida-`
`ble at times, it seems."`

—Kirlilith's unit leaped out from the smoke, ramming their Exelia. Unable to evade, they took the blow at full force and slammed into a nearby tree.

"Kir...lilith...!"

`"You...got lucky. But on the battlefield, those`
`who rely on luck...will die!"`

The enemy Exelia was also heavily damaged, but it still had them beat in terms of sheer horsepower. Its front legs pinned their Exelia, rendering them completely immobile.

The two units were locked together, no longer able to move at all.

"It all...ends here!"

Kirlilith's face appeared behind her windshield. Blood trickled down it from the previous blast, but that was all. They'd only succeeded in wounding her lightly.

"Tch..."

Rain lifted his rifle to fire Bullet Magic.

...Dammit!

But he couldn't see a path to victory. His Qualia told him that no matter where he fired, he wouldn't hit Kirlilith. It seemed the brief openings had disappeared now that she'd started taking him seriously.

"Die."

Kirlilith noticed Rain's momentary lapse and knocked their Exelia off balance with a sideways sweep from her unit's forearm.

Oh no...!

And Rain was dislodged from his seat.

Ah...

His body soared through the air. He reached out to try to grab on to the machine, but he missed the mark. And as he fell down toward the ground, Rain realized he'd lost the gamble.

Shit...!

If he were to hit the ground now, Air would essentially be a sitting duck, with no offensive capabilities of her own. And Rain would have no Exelia.

No, who were they kidding? This match was all but decided already. Rain and Air had lost the moment their sneak attack had failed to finish Kirlilith. That had been their one chance, but they'd flubbed it.

Goddammit...!

Many emotions were at war within him at the moment, but bitter frustration won out. Given the situation, he had no choice but to admit he'd failed. He'd driven both himself and the silver girl to their deaths, leaving nothing to show for it.

However, just as Rain started accepting his death...

Huh...?

...his prediction changed altogether.

What's going on...?

The sense of despair filling him dissipated as his fate changed. Soon enough, he realized what'd happened. Seconds had passed, yet he hadn't hit the ground. And when he lifted his gaze, he understood the reason why.

★   ★   ★

Air had grabbed on to his arm.

"Air...?"

"Quit...daydreaming, you idiot!"

Air had touched him. Air had actually touched Rain. Until this very moment, she'd violently rejected the idea of coming into direct contact with other people. But that same girl was clasping his arm tightly, her skin touching his.

"Air, why...?"

"Why...? Didn't you swear we'd win?!"

Letting go of the steering wheel, Air reached out her free hand and grabbed on to him, refusing to let go.

"You said...you'd change the world, didn't you?" she rasped. "Then your only path forward is to aim and shoot, Rain Lantz!"

Air yanked hard at Rain's arm. She'd just *saved Rain*. And that single act had shifted all his predictions.

"Ah...!"

That near-impossible feat had made the situation entirely unpredictable.

Both for Kirlilith, who'd believed Air would never act to save someone, and for Rain, who hadn't believed Air would touch a person of her own volition.

And more than anyone else, for Air, who'd reacted almost on instinct. Luckily, that single moment, when all their predictions were annulled, was Rain's chance.

...I'll end things here!

Rain unleashed his Bullet Magic straight at Kirlilith. Fire raged through the air, and this time, his spell burned away half of the Ghost's body.

★   ★   ★

"Gh, aaah!"

The blast knocked Kirlilith away. She hadn't died instantly, but there was no way she was getting back up. Rain had seen over half her body burning.

Man, that was even more of a gamble...

The tension finally drained out of him. He'd nearly died several times over because of Kirlilith's overwhelming ability. Nothing he'd tried had worked in the face of her transcendent Qualia and her bullets' incomparable destructive might. But Air never gave up—and they had survived.

All that's left...

Rain reached into his breast pocket and pulled out a silver bullet. He had to finish Kirlilith with it, so he walked up to her body with it in hand.

"I'm...surprised..."

Her voice sounded extremely feeble.

"A Ghost, saving another... And me...losing..."

"Make no mistake—you were way out of my league. If you hadn't toyed with us at the start, you would've won."

"...Yeah...you're right."

As he gazed at her, Rain noticed that the left side of Kirlilith's body was a charred husk.

"At some point, death became...almost unimaginable...," she said. "I've lived for...over a century... I've claimed lives both young and old in battle. I've even killed infants... And then I'd disappear...and wake again for the next battle... In all those many years, I never imagined...I would die like this."

Those were the dying words of the eldest Ghost, Kirlilith Lambert.

★　　★　　★

"I see." Air climbed down from the Exelia and began speaking to her. "In all your prior battles, during all your prior victories, you never truly *feared* death. Right now, you're clinging to life for the very first time."

"That was…what strength meant…to me…," the dying crimson girl said. It was pitiful, truly. "I stole and destroyed…without ever worrying for my own life. That was all I wanted…after I died like an insect…on the battlefield. It was what I wished for the most… as a Ghost… The power I sought in life."

The power she sought in life?

"Say, Air…haven't you…ever resented it?"

"Resented it?"

Air paused for a moment as she considered how to respond. "What about you, Kirlilith? Do you?"

"Of course…I do… All the Ghosts I've met have powers that stem from…their hatred. Inside, they're dark pits of rage…as black as the color of our eyes."

So wasn't Air full of hatred, too? Didn't she loathe the world that had turned them all into terrible monsters?

Air fought back her wasp-hued eyes as she responded to Kirlilith's provocation. "I've heard enough. Rain."

She hadn't answered her question. She hadn't given the dying Kirlilith the word she wanted to hear.

"We're done here. I'll kill Kirlilith…and permanently erase her existence," Air said as she whipped out her own pistol and loaded it with the Devil's Bullet. However—

"Ha-ha-ha."

Even at the very end, Kirlilith laughed. Even here in agony, she was mocking them.

"I don't mind...dying. Honestly, I've grown a bit tired...of living. But..."

And then...

"...I don't want...to have my existence erased."

...at that exact moment...

This is...!

...Rain sensed a massive surge of mana diffusing around the area, washing over the terrain. A symbol surfaced on the ground around them...the Traxil's emblem.

"I am...the Ghost Kirlilith."

The sight came as a shock. If Kirlilith could invoke the spell to blow up the mine so easily, that meant she had prepared it before she ever called them here. And that meant it'd been ready to blow during their entire battle.

So what would happen if all the heat she had accumulated was released at the same time? What if Kirlilith, one of the strongest mages, unleashed all her magic at once?

"I won't let anyone...steal my magic!"

As soon as the words left her mouth, her magic formula activated in exchange for its creator's life.

The Ghost Kirlilith Lambert.

Her final shot had pierced through the bedrock, reached the mine's alloy, and caused a massive explosion.

The entire mine began to crumble and cave inward. The trees caught fire, the terrain shifted, and the raging shock waves scattered mineral dust and ashes, painting the whole area Kirlilith's crimson color in seconds.

And within that raging inferno, the Ghost Air regained consciousness, jolted awake by the spiraling flames.

"Aaah, the fire...!"

Her field of vision swirled and shook as the pain overwhelmed her. Looking down, she realized her left leg was trapped under a large rock.

This is bad...

She tried moving it, but that didn't do anything.

I can't... This is it...

The rock hadn't budged. And unfortunately for her, the flames didn't die down at all as they gradually closed in on her.

Oh.

Air hadn't expected her life to come to an end in such an anticlimactic manner.

I...

She'd tried to think about how many times she'd repeated the cycle of war as a Ghost, about what exactly she'd gained over those endless ages.

......

She'd been sent to the gallows on false charges. And when she'd first awoken as a Ghost, she'd found a peculiar silver bullet in her hands—a silver bullet with the power to change the world. She'd thought that maybe, just maybe, she could use it for good. That perhaps, with that power, she could fix the broken world. But she'd failed.

Why am I so...so...

When she lowered her eyes, her gaze fell on the countless scars on her body.

...so filthy...?

The betrayals from those she'd loved had torn her heart apart. Time after time, she had been plunged into the pits of despair.

I...

After being stabbed in the back so many times, she'd gradually started to fear growing close to anyone, until eventually, the thought of someone touching her body repulsed her. Air had feared the idea so much that she would lash out at anyone who even attempted it. She'd assumed anyone who touched her would see her true, disgusting self.

Air had only gotten over it, just a little, at the very end, when she reached out to save the boy as he fell. It had lasted a mere moment, but her body had moved on instinct and touched him.

What's going on...?

In the end, she'd only managed to conquer that one nasty habit. Air had absolutely nothing else to show for her long life.

Someone…

The flames moved to consume her; they didn't care that she'd never found someone who truly accepted her.

Someone—anyone, it doesn't matter who…

As she drew her last breath, Air decided to put her desires into words.

"Please, save me…"

In that moment, she wasn't a Ghost or some genius mage. She had no appearances to keep up, no reason to hold her tongue. She was just a lonely, wounded girl begging for help. And those pure, honest words…

"There you are."

"Huh…?"

…reached a certain boy's ears.

A familiar voice called out to her from beyond the flames— low, rude, and cold.

"…Hard to find, aren't you?"

"Wh-what…?"

"Why're you acting all confused, Air? We're getting out of here. There's too much fire and smoke."

As he spoke, magic pulverized the rock pinning Air's leg. The boy had fired Bullet Magic within the searing flames, even though he was struggling to breathe himself.

"Why are you still here…?"

"Why? Well, sorry to disappoint you, but this is just a coincidence. I saw that thing on your neck reflecting the flames."

Rain pointed at the object dangling from Air's neck as he said that. It was the silver necklace, the very same one he'd gifted to his younger sister, Rilm, seven years ago.

"It has some alloy inside it, and alloy scatters longer wavelengths of light. Red light, like these flames. That's why I could see it even through the rubble."

Rain picked Air up while he was explaining, and as he carried her on his back, the girl struggled to understand the true meaning of his actions.

Why...?

Rain and Air advanced together through the flames, the latter leaning against the former's back.

"Why...?" Air mumbled out from behind him.

"Huh? Like I said, it was a total coincidence."

"Why did you save me?"

Why did this boy...?

"If I die...you'll be set free..."

When Air had granted him her divinity, she'd also bound him to her with a pact. In exchange for the Devil's Bullet's powers, Rain relinquished the ability to disobey her orders. But part of the agreement was that if she died, he would be freed from that curse.

The cadet Rain Lantz harbored a deep-seated rage within him due to the unjust deaths of his friends and family. The war between the East and the West had claimed everyone he'd ever loved. And Air had taken advantage of those feelings. She'd always known the outcome of giving him the Devil's Bullet.

His anger didn't burn like a flame. It was terribly calm and almost indifferent. It had been obvious to her that he'd use the Devil's Bullet to change the world and conclude their endless war.

That meant that in his eyes, Air and her pact of absolute servitude were nothing but a nuisance.

Of course, Air's own rage wasn't to be trifled with. Nothing had ever wiped that moment from her mind—her unjust execution one hundred years ago. That memory lingered within her, festering like a deep wound.

When she had been reborn as a Ghost and gained the Belial's divinity, there was only a single thought at the forefront of her mind...

I wish everything would just disappear!

And the power she'd gained stemmed from that state of mind.

So I...

She'd used the boy. She'd offered him an appealing power and coerced him into battles between Ghosts. And as a result, the lives of many of his classmates and friends had been forfeited.

"Rain... Did you forget?"

"Forget what?"

"If I die, the pact binding you will dissolve."

She was offering the reminder at the most inopportune moment.

"Huh? How would I forget something that important?"

"So why?"

"You're smart."

"...Huh?" Air mumbled, clearly confused. She thought she might have misheard him.

"Much smarter than I am, really," Rain stated firmly. "Plus, your Exelia handling is crazy good. I totally would've lost that fight with Kirlilith if you weren't around."

He'd given such a simple, practical reason.

"You've got it all backward, Air. I'm the one using you. Don't you die before I'm done."

"That's..."

"And honestly...I feel bad for you, too."

"Ugh..."

"You Ghosts lead pretty tragic lives, huh?"

The flames had spread out so far that every breath burned Rain's lungs, making his voice especially husky.

"You died in the middle of battle, still full of regrets... And every few decades, someone you don't even know resurrects you and forces you to fight, until it's time to start the cycle again... You're like a heat haze, appearing and disappearing at random. It's probably the saddest thing I've ever heard."

Rain's stamina should've been at its limits. He'd depleted his mana reserves during the battle with Kirlilith, so he should've been on the brink of collapse. And yet he never once let his hold on Air slacken. He just resolutely walked on through the raging flames with her on his back.

"Don't you wanna beat the crap out of them, Air?"

"...Huh?"

"Those people who use the dead like toys. Don't you wanna drag them down from their pedestal and beat them to a pulp?"

"Well..."

She obviously did. If Air had simply disappeared one hundred years ago, she wouldn't have been forced to keep fighting in her wounded, blemished body.

"Of course I do..."

"Then don't you dare die!" Rain insisted. He was telling Air to let him save her.

What's with him...?

She'd never met anyone quite like him. In all her time as a Ghost, no one had ever treated her so kindly; no one had ever tried to save her.

I don't understand... You're saving me?

As a ghost, she'd been continually resurrected against her will, and with each life, she gave her bullet to countless different people, taking advantage of them and being taken advantage of in turn. Some were kind to her at first, but the power of the Devil's Bullet soon painted their souls black.

Overwhelming power was fertile soil for greed. And all those who'd grown arrogant upon gaining her power had, without exception, tried to claim her life.

That's...right...

It hadn't just happened once or twice.

All of them...

Every single one of them had tried to erase Air's existence to claim her power. Not all the scars on her body were a result of the battlefield. More than half had been inflicted by former partners, the people she'd granted the Devil's Bullet.

That's just how...people naturally are...

She'd believed in others, entrusting them with her Devil's Bullet. She'd had no choice but to believe in them, because if she hadn't, the solitude would have crushed her. Ghosts lived outside any regular perception of time, so they were often filled with an unbearable loneliness. They had to fight through countless battlefields, claim countless lives all on their own.

Air couldn't handle that, so she'd decided she needed someone by her side. But whenever she'd found someone to help stave off that solitude, they'd betrayed her. Time after time, one trusted companion after another.

I decided to never trust someone again...

Before she knew it, she'd lost faith in humanity as a whole. She'd told Rain as much during her first meeting with the boy during the fourth war.

"If I die, the pact binding you will dissolve."

Any normal person who'd heard such words after receiving the Devil's Bullet would have gone after her, making them easier to read and pacify. However, instead of trying to claim her life, Rain had told her to live and get revenge.

I can't…understand him…at all…

It would've been hard to escape the flames even on his own, yet he still wanted both of them to survive. And that action shook the very foundations of her soul.

Why…?

It broke the seal locking her heart away…

Why am I so…?

…and filled her with warmth from the inside. The feeling was surprisingly hot amid the flames, but it was not at all unpleasant. It was a type of pain she'd never felt before.

What is this…? Something in my chest…feels strange…

And as she leaned into it, the boy's back felt extremely warm.

I…

For some reason, even though she hated being touched, she felt calm instead of agitated. Her body did not reject the boy as she nestled into him.

"Dammit. It's burning over here, too… Where can we even go?"

They'd completely lost their way out as the flames beat at their backs.

"Rain."

"What? We've got no time for chitchat."

"*Let go of me.*"

"Ah!"

The moment Air spoke, Rain's body acted against his wishes to fulfill the order, and he released her. And without his arms holding her up, she dropped straight to the ground. Of course, Rain hadn't intended to let her fall, but he had no choice.

"Ughhh... Ouch... I should've told you to put me down gently..."

"What are you...?"

"Oh, one additional order. *Don't move off that spot.*"

Rain had started to walk over to her, but his legs had suddenly frozen in place. He desperately tried to keep going, but he couldn't even feel his stiff legs. The order had clearly been enhanced with magic. Air had invoked the pact.

"What are you doing...now of all times?"

"There's no escaping the fire at this point."

"That's why we have to find somewhere to hide..."

"Nowhere around here is safe," Air said as she lifted her body using her one good arm and wobbled to her wounded feet. "It's pointless. I have this mine's terrain memorized, so I can tell how far the fire has spread."

The entire area would be engulfed in three minutes.

"And that's why...we have to use the Devil's Bullet," Air stated as she reached a hand to her belt and whipped out her pistol. Of course, the Devil's Bullet changed the world by erasing a person, so they needed a specific target.

Through the flames, Rain saw Air hold on to the gun's grip.

"I finally, finally"—Air paused, then lowered her voice to a whisper—"understand."

"You and I—"

—*are the same.*

They were *extremely* alike. Both of them had once been far too weak to accept the absurdity of war and how quickly lives could be extinguished. But they couldn't remain weak, so they'd sought greater power…and ended up with a burden that no one should've had to bear alone.

A more ordinary person would've buckled under that pressure, but those two still elected to fight. And she'd never met another like her. She'd never met a person who'd understood a Ghost's way of life, *her* way of life.

Within the deadly environment of a battlefield, no one had ever tried to understand Air. Instead, they'd simply deemed her too unlike themselves. But not this boy.

We're the same…

They were completely different people, but they shared something at their core, since they'd shouldered the same burden. And that was why he'd instantly told her to live when she'd accepted her own death.

Seriously…

Air sighed, feeling rather forlorn.

You really are quite pushy. But…

She'd gathered her thoughts and decided to put them into words.

"Now, Rain, listen well."

The boy had fallen to his knees, ready to make the ultimate sacrifice, and the girl proudly stood before him. She knew entrusting the rest of the war to him was unfair, but she also truly believed he'd be fine. She believed he'd succeed, no matter the odds.

"I have a few things I need you to hear."

"What?"

Air's voice was calm but also somewhat playful, much like her usual tone. "First, I want you to end this war at any cost."

Air didn't aim her muzzle at Rain. Instead, the gun moved toward her own temple.

"This is an order you must obey. I want you to stop the war, even though no one's been able to do that over the last one hundred years. It'll be your hardest task, but you must accomplish it. I won't let you refuse. I mean, you even said you'd do it earlier."

The flames drew ever closer to their bodies.

"Second, I want you to make sure you use the Devil's Bullet justly. It's corrupted the heart of every mage before you, but I know you're different. Fight hard."

He'd known something had felt off.

What the hell are you saying, Air?!

But he'd guessed the girl's intentions far too late.

"And third…"

Unfortunately, her order bound him, so he couldn't move.

"Don't forget me."

She looked directly into his eyes as she said that.

"Anyone who has their existence erased is forgotten by everyone aside from the bullet's user. Honestly, I'm not all that attached to this world, but…I suppose I do want to live on inside at least one person… Just a bit, though."

You can't be serious, Air!

She'd ordered him not to move away, but that meant he still had use of his upper body. So Rain pulled out his pistol and shot at the gun in her hands. The feat required incredibly precise aim, but it wasn't at all impossible. His bullet drew a tight arc, heading straight for Air's gun. But…

"Oh, and get stronger, would you?"

…she easily evaded his shot with a slight twist of her body. It was one last message to the boy, spoken through actions instead of words.

"I am the Ghost Air."

This was the end Air herself had chosen as she pressed the barrel of her gun into her throat.

"That's the one thing I don't want you to forget."

And then she fired the silver bullet, the bullet that shifted the world. The next moment, everything distorted, and a distinct sensation ran through Rain's body. It was proof that the Reprogramming had commenced.

The world warped before his very eyes.

"...Air!" he screamed, a desperate cry from a boy who loathed the world just as much as she had.

But the world still transformed...into one where she'd never even existed.

It had been three days since the battle at the Claw Mine. Orca had finally been discharged from the military hospital, but he heard a strange sound on his way out.

"Aaaaaaaaah!"

"What the hell?!"

He jolted in shock. And upon fearfully peeking into the room the sound had come from, he saw someone being pinned down by the nurses.

"St-stop! I-it hurts! I'm fine! I can change them on my own!"

"Hush, you!"

"Last time we let you handle it on your own, you forgot!"

"No, like I keep telling you, I'm— Aaaaaah!"

The cry had come from his classmate Rain, who was kicking and screaming as the staff tried to change his gauze and bandages. He seemed to be throwing a tantrum as two nurses held his legs down and forcibly removed his trousers to disinfect his wound.

Man, he may be some big hotshot out on the battlefield, but this is pathetic...

Orca was disappointed by his behavior. Rain may have moved like a demon during battle, but he was acting like any old bratty child at the moment.

Once they'd finished changing Rain's gauze, Orca entered the room and said, "The scariest part about burns is having the gauze changed, am I right?"

"O-oh, Orca... Man, if you were watching, you could've stepped in and stopped them."

"Let the poor nurses treat you in peace, blockhead."

As he spoke, Orca gave Rain a once-over, and what he saw stunned him. The bases of Rain's thighs were covered in burns, and since he'd only just had his gauze changed, his butt was half-exposed.

He couldn't rest on his back, so his only choice was to remain flat on his stomach, leaving his buttocks exposed to the cold air.

It was quite a...*silly* sight, to be sure.

"Well, if you're not here to visit, then what are you here for?"

"Oh, they're discharging me, so I figured I'd come report my findings."

"Your findings...? Oh, right, the thing I asked you to look into."

"Yeah."

Orca paused for a moment there, and noting that Rain's expression had changed a bit, he added, "I looked into it like you asked, but I couldn't find anything on a person named Kirlilith."

They remained there in silence for a while after he said that.

"Are you sure?"

"Yeah, there were some field officers among the prisoners we rounded up, and none of them knew anyone who went by that name. I mentioned she's a woman with almost unnaturally beautiful red hair, but none of them even knew any female officers, apparently."

"I see."

"Well, in a war as large as this one, ranks change often enough. So..."

Orca paused before asking the question on his mind.

"Who is this Kirlilith anyway?"

"Just someone I met once. I thought I saw her the other day, so I got curious."

"Well, my investigation was pretty sloppy, so I'll check again. It's hard to find information about an enemy country's troops."

With that, Orca left the room, trying not to look at the palm-sized burn Rain had suffered during the last battle.

...So there's nothing, huh?

Rain looked at his own burned, exposed backside.

Kirlilith...

His wounds weren't particularly severe, so he'd been shuffled off to a small hospital that had enough spare beds. Besides, he hadn't exactly been injured in combat...

"I can't believe you sat on an Exelia's engine and burned your butt!"

"Zip it." Rain snapped at a girl who was seated on the other side of the room. He stared at her intently as her distinct *silver hair* shifted around her shoulders. "But, uh, Air...this position's kind of embarrassing. Could you look away for a bit?"

"...Yes, I'll admit I'm not too fond of staring at a person's backside."

The girl looked away and held up her rifle.

"...Just hurry up."

There was a small blush on her face. Apparently, she didn't mind showing off her body, but seeing someone else's was too much for her to handle.

Three days had passed since the battle at the Claw Mine. The greatest mine explosion in recent memory had occurred back there, but that fact had been wiped out of the pages of history by the Reprogramming.

"So the Devil's Bullet *was* involved, then."

"Of course."

The military hospital covered a lot of territory so they could be used for practical training, which left ample space to walk around. And so the artificial mage Rain and the Ghost girl Air walked side by side.

"Back then, I used the Devil's Bullet on myself." Air recalled that moment vividly. "I'm certain I did. But right before I got hit, someone else used the Devil's Bullet to stop the battle at the Claw Mine from ever happening."

It had happened at almost exactly the same moment Air shot herself. The world had distorted and warped, and when Rain came to, he'd been back at Alestra Academy.

At first, he'd thought that was a result of Air's disappearance. Her actions had stirred up a complex storm of emotions within him, and he'd grieved for her. But that same day, Air had appeared out of nowhere with an apologetic expression on her face.

"That was pretty damn awkward."

"Don't mention that, I'm begging you."

Air hated talking about that memory, so Rain chose to move past it.

After reuniting, the two of them had set out for maneuver training and found themselves in another battle, which had ended with just a few injured soldiers. Rain had burned his behind on an Exelia's engine, but that was nothing compared to his injuries from the mine's explosion.

Whatever the case, a Reprogramming definitely had happened, but Air hadn't died, and her existence hadn't been erased.

They'd pondered over how that was possible for quite a while, but only one conclusion came to mind.

"Someone else used the Devil's Bullet. That's the only logical explanation."

"Is that even possible?"

"Yes. After all, pretty much anyone can shoot the bullet as long as they have it. That's how you used it the first time, remember?"

"Yeah, now that you mention it."

"So the question is, who shot whom?"

The girl who'd planned to die back at the mine had begun taking control of her own future a bit more. She'd always floated from one moment to the next, but she'd even been working diligently to figure out what had happened on that day.

"I think we can safely assume Kirlilith got erased."

"Based on Orca's findings, that sounds plausible, but…"

There were no traces of Kirlilith's existence, but Rain still didn't like that hypothesis. After all, he'd seen Kirlilith disappear into the flames with his own two eyes.

"Maybe she played dead?"

"With those injuries?"

"I wouldn't put it past her. I know I'm not one to talk, but Ghosts are obsessed with staying alive. She probably just made a huge spectacle to hide her escape."

That idea was somewhat disappointing, since she'd gone out in a rather noble blaze of glory.

"Whatever the case, we know Kirlilith survived the initial explosion. And even as the flames closed in on us, she was still alive until that very last moment."

"And then someone used the Devil's Bullet to kill her?" Rain asked.

"Right," Air replied. "Think about it. The battle at the mine has been erased, which means the person who got shot was the mastermind behind the whole operation, right? And when we looked into her after the shift, we failed to find a shred of information on Kirlilith. It's evident that she was erased back there."

But in that case, one question still remained unanswered.

"So then who did it?"

"No idea."

That was a complete mystery.

"Someone other than us got their hands on the Devil's Bullet and shot Kirlilith."

"You say that, but where'd they get it? Only you can make that bullet, and only I can create copies."

"Right, which leaves only one option." In Air's mind, it was obvious what had happened. "Someone must've swiped a bullet from you, Rain."

"…Whoa."

Seriously?!

"Or maybe you dropped it somewhere. Either way, someone got the Devil's Bullet off you. I swear, you need to keep an eye on your own belongings."

At her reprimand, Rain found himself at a loss for words and hung his head in disappointment.

"Also, this battle confirmed it. *Someone* is intentionally having us Ghosts fight. In fact…perhaps they've staged this entire war between the East and the West."

That was an oddly ambiguous turn of phrase for Air.

"At first, this whole war started as a battle over alloy. But the more intense the war became, the more alloy the countries ended up using. It's all pointless. Everything mined goes into military production, so they're essentially just fighting for the privilege of fighting more, and this cycle's lasted over a hundred years. It makes no sense."

Meaning there was someone orchestrating events behind the scenes. And as long as that person remained in power, the war would never truly come to an end.

......

That person, whoever they may be, was their real target. And Rain shivered ever so slightly as he thought of them.

"...But we'll cross that bridge when we come to it," Air said dismissively. "Listen to me, Rain..."

The Ghost girl had recently tried to end her own life, but she'd survived by some twist of fate—her existence was an unstable one indeed.

"The war between the East and the West isn't even close to its end."

On her back, she carried two comically large rifles. No one would've ever believed that such a tiny girl had granted him the power to change the world.

"Can you still fight?"

Their gazes met.

"We have many reasons for fighting, and there's a lot that stands in our way, but when we overcome all those obstacles, our dreams will come true."

As Air spoke, she threw a lone silver bullet his way. It reflected myriad rays from the sun behind her, and yet, its silver gleam remained unblemished.

"Of course. My feelings haven't changed one bit since the moment I first took hold of your Devil's Bullet."

"I see."

His answer had been firm and unyielding, which caught the girl off guard.

I swear… He really is…

She felt some bewilderment rise up within her as she thought of all he'd done for her. However, the conversation did not end there.

"Listen, Air, if we're gonna do this, I want you to promise me one thing."

"Oh?"

"Never pull another one of those suicide stunts again."

"That's…"

"A gunner looks for much more than just mutual trust when choosing an Exelia partner. They have to have resilience. They have to avoid death and cling to life, even if it means getting on their hands and knees and eating mud and filth. Gunners put their lives in the hands of their manipulators because of that. And that means from now on, you can't ever give up on life again."

That was Rain's one and only request.

"As long as you promise me that, I'll even be your slave."

"…But a slave isn't what I want."

Air cocked her head to one side.

"A partner will do just fine, I suppose."

And then the Ghost Air looked his way and smiled.

"Ah…"

The expression on her face was something Rain had never seen before. It wasn't a scoffing smirk or a wry smile. It was a pure, lovely…honestly adorable smile. He could tell she felt bashful… and just a bit happy.

Yeah...

Her smile was *extremely* cute.

Yeah, this...

Rain could tell she was expressing her real feelings. It had nothing to do with Ghosts, mysterious bullets, or abnormal divinities. For the first time, he'd managed to see a part of her true self.

"...Well, let's put that aside for now."

"Yes, we need to strategize for the next battle."

For the moment, that was their top priority. They still had to find the person who'd stolen the missing Devil's Bullet, and even besides that, there was plenty else left to do. And so they started to discuss what they'd do following Rain's discharge.

Slowly, and with great leisure, the two of them walked onward...together.

Meanwhile...

Orca entered the Exelia hangar and, after a quick search, found the girl he'd planned to meet there.

"Athly."

"Yeah...?" Athly responded as she moved her eyes off her Exelia. "Oh, did I call you over?"

"You asked me to look into this!"

It seemed she'd completely forgotten. Everyone always assumed she was a responsible person, but she was actually an airhead a lot of the time.

"...Well, whatever. Here's the info you wanted."

"Thanks."

Orca handed Athly the bundle of documents she'd requested. And then he added, "Man...talk about weird coincidences."

"Weird coincidences?"

"Hmm… You both asked me separately, so I was gonna keep it a secret…"

Orca seemed conflicted over the issue, unsure whether he should say anything.

"Well, I guess it probably doesn't matter."

But eventually, he brushed aside his hesitation and decided to continue talking.

"Both of you asked me to look into this Kirlilith person, so where's the harm, right?"

"Both…? You mean someone else asked about her?"

"Yeah. Rain."

At that point, Orca finally got a good look at the girl standing in front of him. And as he did, he noticed that she looked rather thin and sickly.

"The two of you asked about her three days ago. What, is she some celebrity I don't know?"

"…A celebrity, huh?" Athly set down the Exelia calibration tool beside her.

She'd been tending to the unit she'd ridden through countless battlefields to keep it functional. It was standard procedure, and a mage's bullets and guns needed similar care.

"Maybe, of a sort."

Athly, the girl who'd lost her parents in the attack on Leminus, reached into her breast pocket and pulled out a single shell. Its vivid colors had faded, but it was still obviously the shell of a *silver bullet* with the letters of a person's name etched onto it:

"She's gone now, though."

Kirlilith Lambert.

Hello, everyone. This is Kei Uekawa.

I sincerely thank you for picking up my novel.

First, I'd like to talk a little about the book itself.

This whole book is based on the concept of magic bullets, but originally, the term was used to describe penicillin, the first antibiotic discovered by mankind. Due to its effectiveness and its ability to target diseases without harming the patient, it was described as a "magic bullet."

The idea was also featured in Carl Maria von Weber's opera *Der Freischütz*, in which six out of seven bullets hit with perfect accuracy, while the seventh was bound to the devil's intentions.

The Devil's Bullet featured in this story draws inspiration from both of those sources.

Now let's move on to some acknowledgments.

I've made it this far only thanks to the many people who decided to take a chance on my work. This novel came in first at the 31st Fantasia Awards, but it didn't get there through my efforts alone. TEDDY was responsible for the illustrations, Naohiro Washio was in charge of the Exelia's designs, and many people at the editorial department helped me polish up my work enough to appeal to the judges. I've received a great deal of help from all of them.

Thank you all so, so much. And most importantly, thank you, dear readers, for choosing to pick up this book.

What will become of our protagonist and the Devil's Bullet? I can only hope you keep reading to find out.

Well then, let's meet again in the next book.

Kei Uekawa

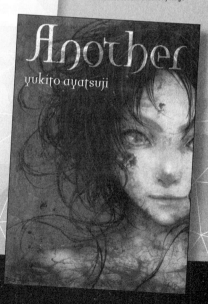

Our Last CRUSADE
OR THE RISE OF A
New World

LIGHT NOVEL

MANGA

AVAILABLE NO
WHEREVER BOO
ARE SOL

LOVE IS A
BATTLEFIELD

When a princess and a knight from rival nations
fall in love, will they find a way to end a war
or remain star-crossed lovers forever...?

For more informa
visit www.yenpress.com